JERRY JUNIOR

By

JEAN WEBSTER

First published in 1907

This edition published by Read Books Ltd.

British Library Cataloguing-in-Publication Data
A catalogue record for this book is available
from the British Library

CONTENTS

ILLUSTRATIONS

Jean Webster

Alice Jane Chandler Webster, perhaps better known under her pseudonym Jean Webster, was born on 24 July 1876, at Fredonia, New York, USA. She was the eldest child of Annie Moffet Webster and Charles Luther Webster, and spent her early childhood in a strongly matriarchal and activist setting. Her great-grandmother, grandmother and mother all lived under the same roof; her great-grandmother working on temperance issues, and her grandmother on racial equality and women's suffrage. Webster herself remained a lifelong supporter of women's suffrage and children's institutional reform. Alice's mother was niece to Mark Twain, and her father was Twain's business manager and subsequently publisher of many of his books. Unfortunately, the company ran into difficulties, after which her father had a nervous breakdown and leave of absence. He subsequently committed suicide in 1891 from a drug overdose.

Alice attended the Fredonia Normal School and graduated in 1894 in china painting, thereafter attending the Lady Jane Grey School in Binghamton from 1894-96. It was this latter establishment which provided the inspiration for Webster's later novel, *Just Patty* (published 1911). In 1897, Webster entered Vassar College. Majoring in English and economics, she also took courses in welfare and penal reform, and from this point on became heavily involved in improving the living conditions in institutions for delinquent and destitute children. After her graduation in 1901, Webster began writing *When Patty Went to College,* in which she described contemporary women's college life. It was published in 1903, to good reviews, which spurred her on to copmplete her second novel *The Wheat Princess,* published in 1905. In the following years, Webster embarked on an eight month world tour to Burma, China, Egypt, Hong Kong,

India, Indonesia, Japan and Sri Lanka with her friends Ethelyn McKinney, Lena Weinstein and two others, as well as writing *Jerry Junior* in 1907 and *The Four Pools Mystery* in 1908.

Webster's most famous novel, *Daddy-Long-Legs*, was written in less exotic settings however; whilst the author was staying at an old farmhouse in Tyringham, Massachusetts. It tells the story of an orphaned girl, 'Judy' whose attendance at a women's college is sponsored by an anonymous benefactor. The novel takes the form of letters written by the young lady to her sponsor, and met popular and critical acclaim on its release in 1912. Webster later dramatized the work, and spent a substantial amount of time on tour with the play, which starred a young Ruth Chatterton as 'Judy'. In her personal life, Webster was greatly delighted, when, at the age of thirty nine, she was able to marry her long-held love, Glenn Ford McKinney. The marriage had hitherto been prevented due to the expectations of the groom's wealthy and successful father – who had forced the young man into an unhappy marriage with Annette Reynaud. Reynaud and McKinney were granted their divorce in 1915, which meant that he and Webster were able to marry in a quiet ceremony in Washington, Connecticut. They honeymooned in Canada, where they were visited by former president Theodore Roosevelt, who invited himself saying, 'I've always wanted to meet Jean Webster. We can put up a partition in the cabin!' On their return to New York, Webster published *Dear Enemy* (1915), a sequel to *Daddy-Long-Legs*, which also proved to be a bestseller. Later that year, Webster was elated to discover she was pregnant, but was warned the pregnancy might be dangerous due to a history of difficult births in the family. Her friends reported that they had never seen her happier; she suffered severely from morning sickness, but was better by February 1916. She entered the Sloan Hospital for Women, New York on 10 June 1916, and gave birth to a healthy daughter. Unfortunately, despite a positive outlook at first, Webster became ill and died of childbirth fever the following day. Her daughter was named Jean in her honour.

"Constance studied the mountains a moment"

JERRY JUNIOR

CHAPTER I

The courtyard of the Hotel du Lac, furnished with half a dozen tables and chairs, a red and green parrot chained to a perch, and a shady little arbor covered with vines, is a pleasant enough place for morning coffee, but decidedly too sunny for afternoon tea. It was close upon four of a July day, when Gustavo, his inseparable napkin floating from his arm, emerged from the cool dark doorway of the house and scanned the burning vista of tables and chairs. He would never, under ordinary circumstances, have interrupted his siesta for the mere delivery of a letter; but this particular letter was addressed to the young American man, and young American men, as every head waiter knows, are an unreasonably impatient lot. The court-yard was empty, as he might have foreseen, and he was turning with a patient sigh towards the long arbor that led to the lake, when the sound of a rustling paper in the summer house deflected his course. He approached the doorway and looked inside.

The young American man, in white flannels with a red guide-book protruding from his pocket, was comfortably stretched in a lounging chair engaged with a cigarette and a copy of the Paris *Herald*. He glanced up with a yawn—excusable under the circumstances—but as his eye fell upon the letter he sprang to his feet.

"Hello, Gustavo! Is that for me?"

"'Hello, Gustavo! Is that for me?'"

Gustavo bowed.

"*Ecco*! She is at last arrive, ze lettair for which you haf so moch weesh." He bowed a second time and presented it. "Meestair Jayreen Ailyar!"

The young man laughed.

"I don't wish to hurt your feelings, Gustavo, but I'm not sure I should answer if my eyes were shut."

He picked up the letter, glanced at the address to make sure—the name was Jerymn Hilliard Jr.—and ripped it open with an exaggerated sigh of relief. Then he glanced up and caught Gustavo's expression. Gustavo came of a romantic race; there was a gleam of sympathetic interest in his eye.

"Oh, you needn't look so knowing! I suppose you think this is a love letter? Well it's not. It is, since you appear to be interested, a letter from my sister informing me that they will arrive tonight, and that we will pull out for Riva by the first boat tomorrow morning. Not that I want to leave you, Gustavo, but—Oh, thunder!"

He finished the reading in a frowning silence while the waiter stood at polite attention, a shade of anxiety in his eye—there was usually anxiety in his eye when it rested on Jerymn Hilliard Jr. One could never foresee what the young man would call for next. Yesterday he had rung the bell and demanded a partner to play lawn tennis, as if the hotel kept partners laid away in drawers like so many sheets.

He crumpled up the letter and stuffed it in his pocket.

"I say, Gustavo, what do you think of this? They're going to stay in Lucerne till the tenth—that's next week—and they hope I don't mind waiting; it will be nice for me to have a rest. A *rest*, man, and I've already spent three days in Valedolmo!"

"*Si*, signore, you will desire ze same room?" was as much as Gustavo thought.

"Ze same room? Oh, I suppose so."

He sank back into his chair and plunged his hands into his pockets with an air of sombre resignation. The waiter hovered over him, divided between a desire to return to his siesta, and a sympathetic interest in the young man's troubles. Never before in the history of his connection with the Hotel du Lac had Gustavo experienced such a munificent, companionable, expansive, entertaining, thoroughly unique and inexplicable guest. Even the fact that he was American scarcely accounted for everything.

The young man raised his head and eyed his companion gloomily.

"Gustavo, have you a sister?"

"A sister?" Gustavo's manner was uncomprehending but patient. "*Si*, signore, I have eight sister."

"Eight! Merciful saints. How do you manage to be so cheerful?"

"Tree is married, signore, one uvver is betrofed, one is in a convent, one is dead and two is babies."

"I see—they're pretty well disposed of; but the babies will grow up, Gustavo, and as for that betrothed one, I should still be a little nervous if I were you; you can never be sure they are going to stay betrothed. I hope she doesn't spend her time chasing over the map of Europe making appointments with you to meet her in unheard of little mountain villages where the only approach to Christian reading matter is a Paris *Herald* four days old, and then doesn't turn up to keep her appointments?"

Gustavo blinked. His supple back achieved another bow.

"Sank you," he murmured.

"And you don't happen to have an aunt?"

"An aunt, signore?" There was vagueness in his tone.

"Yes, Gustavo, an aunt. A female relative who reads you like an open book, who sees your faults and skips your virtues, who remembers how dear and good and obliging your father was at your age, who hoped great things of you when you were a baby, who had intended to make you her heir but has about decided to endow an orphan asylum—have you, Gustavo, by chance an aunt?"

"*Si*, signore."

"I do not think you grasp my question. An *aunt*—the sister of your father, or perhaps your mother."

A gleam of illumination swept over Gustavo's troubled features.

"*Ecco*! You would know if I haf a *zia*—a aunt—yes, zat is it. A aunt. *Sicuramente*, signore, I haf ten—leven aunt."

"Eleven aunts! Before such a tragedy I am speechless; you need say no more, Gustavo, from this moment we are friends."

He held out his hand. Gustavo regarded it dazedly; then, since it seemed to be expected, he gingerly presented his own. The result was a shining newly-minted two-lire piece. He pocketed it with a fresh succession of bows.

"*Grazie tanto*! Has ze signore need of anysing?"

"Have I need of anysing?" There was reproach, indignation, disgust in the young man's tone. "How can you ask such a question, Gustavo? Here am I, three days in Valedolmo, with seven more stretching before me. I have plenty of towels and soap and soft-boiled eggs, if that is what you mean; but a man's spirit cannot be nourished on soap and soft-boiled eggs. What I need is food for the mind—diversion, distraction, amusement—no,

Gustavo, you needn't offer me the Paris *Herald* again. I already know by heart the list of guests in every hotel in Switzerland."

"Ah, it is diversion zat you wish? Have you seen zat ver' beautiful Luini in ze chapel of San Bartolomeo? It is four hundred years old."

"Yes, Gustavo, I have seen the Luini in the chapel of San Bartolomeo. I derived all the pleasure to be got out of it the first afternoon I came."

"Ze garden of Prince Sartonio-Crevelli? Has ze signore seen ze cedar of Lebanon in ze garden of ze prince?"

"Yes, Gustavo, the signore has seen the cedar of Lebanon in the garden of the prince, also the ilex tree two hundred years old and the india-rubber plant from South America. They are extremely beautiful but they don't last a week."

"Have you swimmed in ze lake?"

"It is lukewarm, Gustavo."

The waiter's eyes roved anxiously. They lighted on the lunette of shimmering water and purple mountains visible at the farther end of the arbor.

"Zere is ze view," he suggested humbly. "Ze view from ze water front is consider ver' beautiful, ver' nice. Many foreigners come entirely for him. You can see Lago di Garda, Monte Brione, Monte Baldo wif ze ruin castle of ze Scaliger, Monte Maggiore, ze Altissimo di Nago, ze snow cover peak of Monte—"

Mr. Jerymn Hilliard Jr. stopped him with a gesture.

"That will do; I read Baedeker myself, and I saw them all the first night I came. You must know at your age, Gustavo, that a man can't enjoy a view by himself; it takes two for that sort of thing—Yes, the truth is that I am lonely. You can see yourself to what straits I am pushed for conversation. If I had your command of language, now, I would talk to the German Alpine climbers."

An idea flashed over Gustavo's features.

"Ah, zat is it! Why does not ze signore climb mountains? Ver' helful; ver' diverting. I find guide."

"You needn't bother. Your guide would be Italian, and it's

too much of a strain to talk to a man all day in dumb show." He folded his arms with a weary sigh. "A week of Valedolmo! An eternity!"

Gustavo echoed the sigh. Though he did not entirely comprehend the trouble, still he was of a generously sympathetic nature.

"It is a pity," he observed casually, "zat you are not acquaint wif ze Signor Americano who lives in Villa Rosa. He also finds Valedolmo undiverting. He comes—but often—to talk wif me. He has fear of forgetting how to spik Angleesh, he says."

The young man opened his eyes.

"What are you talking about—a Signor Americano here in Valedolmo?"

"*Sicuramente*, in zat rose-color villa wif ze cypress trees and ze *terrazzo* on ze lake. His daughter, la Signorina Costantina, she live wif him—ver' yong, ver' beautiful—" Gustavo rolled his eyes and clasped his hands—"beautiful like ze angels in Paradise—and she spik Italia like I spik Angleesh."

Jerymn Hilliard Jr. unfolded his arms and sat up alertly.

"You mean to tell me that you had an American family up your sleeve all this time and never said a word about it?" His tone was stern.

"*Scusi*, signore, I have not known zat you have ze plaisir of zer acquaintance."

"The pleasure of their acquaintance! Good heavens, Gustavo, when one ship-wrecked man meets another ship-wrecked man on a desert island must they be introduced before they can speak?"

"*Si*, signore."

"And why, may I ask, should an intelligent American family be living in Valedolmo?"

"I do not know, signore. I have heard ze Signor Papa's healf was no good, and ze doctors in Americk' zay say to heem, 'you need change, to breave ze beautiful climate of Italia.' And he say, 'all right, I go to Valedolmo.' It is small, signore, but ver' *famosa*. Oh, yes, *molto famosa*. In ze autumn and ze spring foreigners come from all ze world—Angleesh, French, German—*tutti*! Ze Hotel du Lac is full. Every day we turn peoples away."

"So! I seem to have struck the wrong season.—But about this American family, what's their name?"

"La familia Veeldair from Nuovo York."

"Veeldair." He shook his head. "That's not American, Gustavo, at least when you say it. But never mind, if they come from New York it's all right. How many are there—just two?"

"But no! Ze papa and ze signorina and ze—ze—" he rolled his eyes in search of the word—"ze aunt!"

"Another aunt! The sky appears to be raining aunts today. What does she do for amusement—the signorina who is beautiful as the angels?"

Gustavo spread out his hands.

"Valedolmo, signore, is on ze frontier. It is—what you say—garrison *città*. Many soldiers, many officers—captains, lieutenants, wif uniforms and swords. Zay take tea on ze *terrazzo* wif ze Signor Papa and ze Signora Aunt, and most *specialmente* wif ze Signorina Costantina. Ze Signor Papa say he come for his healf, but if you ask me, I sink maybe he come to marry his daughter."

"I see! And yet, Gustavo, American papas are generally not so keen as you might suppose about marrying their daughters to foreign captains and lieutenants even if they have got uniforms and swords. I shouldn't be surprised if the Signor Papa were just a little nervous over the situation. It seems to me there might be an opening for a likely young fellow speaking the English language, even if he hasn't a uniform and sword. How does he strike you?"

"*Si*, signore."

"I'm glad you agree with me. It is now five minutes past four; do you think the American family would be taking a siesta?"

"I do not know, signore." Gustavo's tone was still patient.

"And whereabouts is the rose-colored villa with the terrace on the lake?"

"It is a quarter of a hour beyond ze Porta Sant' Antonio. If ze gate is shut you ring at ze bell and Giuseppe will open. But ze road is ver' hot and ver' dusty. It is more cooler to take ze paf by ze lake. Straight to ze left for ten minutes and step over ze wall; it is broken in zat place and quite easy."

"Thank you, that is a wise suggestion; I shall step over the wall by all means." He jumped to his feet and looked about for his hat. "You turn to the left and straight ahead for ten minutes? Good-bye then till dinner. I go in search of the Signorina Costantina who is beautiful as the angels in Paradise, and who lives in a rose-colored villa set in a cypress grove on the shores of Lake Garda—not a bad setting for romance, is it, Gustavo?—Dinner, I believe, is at seven o'clock?"

"*Si*, signore, at seven; and would you like veal cooked Milanese fashion?"

"Nothing would please me more. We have only had veal Milanese fashion five times since I came."

He waved his hand jauntily and strolled whistling down the arbor that led to the lake. Gustavo looked after him and shook his head. Then he took out the two-lire piece and rang it on the table. The metal rang true. He shrugged his shoulders and turned back indoors to order the veal.

CHAPTER II

The terrace of Villa Rosa juts out into the lake, bordered on three sides by a stone parapet, and shaded above by a yellow-ochre awning. Masses of oleanders hang over the wall and drop pink petals into the blue waters below. As a study in color the terrace is perfect, but, like the court-yard of the Hotel du Lac, decidedly too hot for mid-afternoon. To the right of the terrace, however, is a shady garden set in alleys of cypress trees, and separated from the lake by a strip of beach and a low balustrade. There could be no better resting place for a warm afternoon.

It was close upon four—five minutes past to be accurate—and the usual afternoon quiet that enveloped the garden had fled before the garrulous advent of four girls. Three of them, with black eyes and blacker hair, were kneeling on the beach thumping and scrubbing a pile of linen. In spite of their chatter they were working busily, and the grass beyond the water-wall was already white with bleaching sheets, while a lace trimmed petticoat fluttered from a near-by oleander, and a row of silk stockings stretched the length of the parapet. The most undeductive observer would have guessed by this time that the pink villa, visible through the trees, contained no such modern conveniences as stationary tubs.

The fourth girl, with gray eyes and yellow-brown hair, was sitting at ease on the balustrade, fanning herself with a wide brimmed hat and dangling her feet, clad in white tennis shoes, over the edge. She wore a suit of white linen cut sailor fashion, low at the throat and with sleeves rolled to the elbows. She looked very cool and comfortable and free as she talked, with the utmost friendliness, to the three girls below. Her Italian, to an unaccustomed ear, was exactly as glib as theirs.

"The fourth girl, with gray eyes and yellow-brown hair, was sitting at ease on the balustrade"

The washer-girls were dressed in the gayest of peasant clothes—green and scarlet petticoats, flowered kerchiefs, coral beads and flashing earrings; you would have to go far into the hills in these degenerate days before meeting their match on an Italian highway. But the girl on the wall, who was actual if not titular ruler of the domain of Villa Rosa, possessed a keen eye for effect; and—she plausibly argued—since one must have washer-women about, why not, in the name of all that is beautiful, have them in harmony with tradition and the landscape? Accordingly, she designed and purchased their costumes herself.

There drifted presently into sight from around the little promontory that hid the village, a blue and white boat with yellow lateen sails. She was propelled gondolier fashion, for the wind was a mere breath, by a picturesque youth in a suit of dark blue with white sash and flaring collar —the hand of the girl on the wall was here visible also.

The boat fluttering in toward shore, looked like a giant butterfly; and her name, emblazoned in gold on her prow, was, appropriately, the *Farfalla.* Earlier in the season, with a green hull and a dingy brown sail, she had been prosaically enough, the *Maria.* But since the advent of the girl all this had been changed. The *Farfalla* dropped her yellow wings with the air of a salute, and lighted at the foot of the water-steps under the terrace. The girl on the parapet leaned forward eagerly.

"Did you get any mail, Giuseppe?" she called.

"*Si,* signorina." He scrambled up the steps and presented a copy of the London *Times.*

She received it with a shrug. Clearly, she felt little interest in the London *Times.* Giuseppe took himself back to his boat and commenced fussing about its fittings, dusting the seats, plumping up the cushions, with an air of absorption which deceived nobody. The signorina watched him a moment with amused comprehension, then she called peremptorily:

"Giuseppe, you know you must spade the garden border."

Poor Giuseppe, in spite of his nautical costume, was man of all work. He glanced dismally toward the garden border which lay basking in the sunshine under the wall that divided Villa Rosa from the rest of the world. It contained every known flower which blossoms in July in the kingdom of Italy from camellias and hydrangeas to heliotrope and wall flowers. Its spading was a complicated business and it lay too far off to permit of conversation. Giuseppe was not only a lazy, but also a social soul.

"Signorina," he suggested, "would you not like a sail?"

She shook her head. "There is not wind enough and it is too hot and too sunny."

"But yes, there's a wind, and cool—when you get out on the lake. I will put up the awning, signorina, the sun shall not touch you."

She continued to shake her head and her eyes wandered suggestively to the hydrangeas, but Giuseppe still made a feint of preoccupation. Not being a cruel mistress, she dropped the subject, and turned back to her conversation with the washer-girls. They were discussing—a pleasant topic for a sultry summer afternoon—the probable content of Paradise. The three girls were of the opinion that it was made up of warm sunshine and cool shade, of flowers and singing birds and sparkling waters, of blue skies and cloud-capped mountains—not unlike, it will be observed, the very scene which at the moment stretched before them. In so much they were all agreed, but there were several debatable points. Whether the stones were made of gold, and whether the houses were not gold too, and, that being the case, whether it would not hurt your eyes to look at them. Marietta declared, blasphemously, as the others thought, that she preferred a simple gray stone villa or at most one of pink stucco, to all the golden edifices that Paradise contained.

"Giuseppe still made a feint of preoccupation"

It was by now fifteen minutes past four, and a spectator had arrived, though none of the five were aware of his presence. The spectator was standing on the wall above the garden border examining with appreciation the idyllic scene below him, and with most particular appreciation, the dainty white-clad person of the girl on the balustrade. He was wondering—anxiously—how he might make his presence known. For no very tangible reason he had suddenly become conscious that the matter would be easier if he carried in his pocket a letter of introduction. The purlieus of Villa Rosa in no wise resembled a desert island; and in the face of that very fluent Italian, the suspicion was forcing itself upon him that after all, the mere fact of a common country was not a sufficient bond of union. He had definitely decided to withdraw, when the matter was taken from his hands.

The wall—as Gustavo had pointed out—was broken; it was owing to this fact that he had been so easily able to climb it. Now, as he stealthily turned, preparing to re-descend in the direction whence he had come, the loose stone beneath his foot slipped and he slipped with it. Five startled pairs of eyes were turned in his direction. What they saw, was a young man in flannels suddenly throw up his arms, slide into an azalea bush, from this to the balustrade, and finally land on all fours on the narrow strip of beach, a shower of pink petals and crumbling masonry falling about him. A momentary silence followed; then the washer-girls, making sure that he was not injured, broke into a shrill chorus of laughter, while the *Farfalla* rocked under impact of Giuseppe's mirth. The girl on the wall alone remained grave.

The young man picked himself up, restored his guide book to his pocket, and blushingly stepped forward, hat in hand, to make an apology. One knee bore a splash of mud, and his tumbled hair was sprinkled with azalea blossoms.

"I beg your pardon," he stammered, "I didn't mean to come so suddenly; I'm afraid I broke your wall."

The girl dismissed the matter with a polite gesture.

"It was already broken," and then she waited with an air of grave attention until he should state his errand.

"I—I came—" He paused and glanced about vaguely; he could not at the moment think of any adequate reason to account for his coming.

"Yes?"

Her eyes studied him with what appeared at once a cool and an amused scrutiny. He felt himself growing red beneath it.

"Can I do anything for you?" she prompted with the kind desire of putting him at his ease.

"Thank you—" He grasped at the first idea that presented itself. "I'm stopping at the Hotel du Lac and Gustavo, you know, told me there was a villa somewhere around here that belongs to Prince Someone or Other. If you ring at the gate and give the gardener two francs and a visiting card, he will let you walk around and look at the trees."

"I see!" said the girl, "and so now you are looking for the gate?" Her tone suggested that she suspected him of trying to avoid both it and the two francs. "Prince Sartorio-Crevelli's villa is about half a mile farther on."

"Ah, thank you," he bowed a second time, and then added out of the desperate need of saying something, "There's a cedar of Lebanon in it and an India rubber plant from South America."

"Indeed!"

She continued to observe him with polite interest, though she made no move to carry on the conversation.

"You—are an American?" he asked at length.

"Oh, yes," she agreed easily. "Gustavo knows that."

He shifted his weight.

"I am an American too," he observed.

"Really?" The girl leaned forward and examined him more closely, an innocent, candid, wholly detached look in her eyes. "From your appearance I should have said you were German—most of the foreigners who visit Valedolmo are German."

"Well, I'm not," he said shortly. "I'm American."

"It is a pity my father is not at home," she returned, "*he* enjoys meeting Americans."

A gleam of anger replaced the embarrassment in the young man's eyes. He glanced about for a dignified means of escape; they had him pretty well penned in. Unless he wished to reclimb the wall—and he did not—he must go by the terrace which retreat was cut off by the washer-women, or by the parapet, already occupied by the girl in white and the washing. He turned abruptly and his elbow brushed a stocking to the ground.

He stooped to pick it up and then he blushed still a shade deeper.

"This is washing day," observed the girl with a note of apology. She rose to her feet and stood on the top of the parapet while she beckoned to Giuseppe, then she turned and looked down upon the young man with an expression of frank amusement. "I hope you will enjoy the cedar of Lebanon and the India rubber tree. Good afternoon."

She jumped to the ground and crossed to the water-steps where Giuseppe, with a radiant smile, was steadying the boat against the landing. She settled herself comfortably among the cushions and then for a moment glanced back towards shore.

"You would better go out by the gate," she called. "The wall on the farther side is harder to climb than the one you came in by; and besides, it has broken glass on the top."

Giuseppe raised the yellow sail and the *Farfalla* with a graceful dip, glided out to sea. The young man stood eyeing its progress revengefully. Now that the girl was out of hearing, a number of pointed things occurred to him which he might have said. His thoughts were interrupted by a fresh giggle from behind and he found that the three washer-girls were laughing at him.

"Your mistress's manners are not the best in the world," said he, severely, "and I am obliged to add that yours are no better."

They giggled again, though there was no malice behind their humor; it was merely that they found the lack of a language in common a mirth-provoking circumstance. Marietta, with a flash of black eyes, murmured something very kindly in Italian, as she shook out a linen sailor suit—the exact twin of the one that had gone to sea—and spread it on the wall to dry.

The young man did not linger for further words. Setting his hat firmly on his head, he vaulted the parapet and strode off down the cypress alley that stretched before him; he passed the pink villa without a glance. At the gate he stood aside to admit a horse and rider. The horse was prancing in spite of the heat; the rider wore a uniform and a shining sword. There was a clank of accoutrements as he passed, and the wayfarer caught a gleam of piercing black eyes and a slight black moustache turned up at the ends. The rider saluted politely and indifferently, and jangled on. The young man scowled after him maliciously until the cypresses hid him from view; then he turned and took up the dusty road back towards the Hotel du Lac.

It was close upon five, and Gustavo was in the court-yard feeding the parrot, when his eye fell upon the American guest scuffling down the road in a cloud of white dust. Gustavo hastened to the gate to welcome him back, his very eyebrows expressive of his eagerness for news.

"You are returned, signore?"

The young man paused and regarded him unemotionally.

"Yes, Gustavo, I am returned—with thanks."

"You have seen ze Signorina Costantina?"

"Yes, I saw her."

"And is it not as I have said, zat she is beautiful as ze holy angels?"

"Yes, Gustavo, she is—and just about equally remote. You may make out my bill."

The waiter's face clouded.

"You do not wish to remain longer, signore?"

"Can't stand it, Gustavo; it's too infernally restful."

Poor Gustavo saw a munificent shower of tips vanishing into nothing. His face was rueful but his manner was undiminishingly polite.

"*Si*, signore, sank you. When shall you wish ze omnibus?"

"Tomorrow morning for the first boat."

Gustavo bowed to the inevitable; and the young man passed on. He paused half way across the court-yard.

"What time does the first boat leave?"

"At half past five, signore."
"Er—no—I'll take the second."
"*Si*, signore. At half-past ten."

CHAPTER III

It was close upon ten when Jerymn Hilliard Jr., equipped for travel in proper blue serge, appeared in the doorway of the Hotel du Lac. He looked at his watch and discovered that he still had twenty minutes before the omnibus meeting the second boat was due. He strolled across the court-yard, paused for a moment to tease the parrot, and sauntered on to his favorite seat in the summer house. He had barely established himself with a cigarette when who should appear in the gateway but Miss Constance Wilder of Villa Rosa and a middle-aged man—at a glance the Signor Papa. Jerymn Hilliard's heart doubled its beat. Why, he asked himself excitedly, *why* had they come?

The Signor Papa closed his green umbrella, and having dropped into a chair—obligingly near the summer house—took off his hat and fanned himself. He had a tendency toward being stout and felt the heat. The girl, meanwhile, crossed the court and jangled the bell; she waited two—three—minutes, then she pulled the rope again.

"Gustavo! Oh, Gustavo!"

The bell might have been rung by any-one—the fisherman, the omnibus-driver, Suor Celestina from the convent asking her everlasting alms—and Gustavo took his time. But the voice was unmistakable; he waited only to throw a clean napkin over his arm before hurrying to answer.

"*Buon giorno*, signorina! Good morning, signore. It is beautiful wea-thir, but warm. *Già*, it is warm."

He bowed and smiled and rubbed his hands together. His moustaches, fairly bristling with good will, turned up in a half circle until they caressed his nose on either side. He bustled about placing table and chairs, and recklessly dusting them with the clean napkin. The signorina laid her fluffy white parasol on one chair and seated herself on another, her profile turned to the summer house. Gustavo hovered over them, awaiting their pleasure, the genius itself of respectful devotion. It was Constance who gave the order—she, it might be noticed, gave most of the orders that were given in her vicinity. She framed it in English out of deference to Gustavo's pride in his knowledge of the language.

"A glass of *vino santo* for the Signore and *limonata* for me. I wish to put the sugar in myself, the last time you mixed it, Gustavo, it was all sugar and no lemon. And bring a bowl of cracked ice—*fino*—*fino*—and some pine nut cakes if you are sure they are fresh."

"Sank you, signorina. *Subitissimo*!"

He was off across the court, his black coat-tails, his white napkin streaming behind, proclaiming to all the world that he was engaged on the Signorina Americana's bidding; for persons of lesser note he still preserved a measure of dignity.

The young man in the summer house had meanwhile dropped his cigarette upon the floor and noiselessly stepped on it. He had also—with the utmost caution lest the chair creak—shifted his position so that he might command the profile of the girl. The entrance to the summer house was fortunately on the other side, and in all likelihood they would not have occasion to look within. It was eavesdropping of course, but he had already been convicted of that yesterday, and in any case it was not such very bad eavesdropping. The court-yard of the Hotel du Lac was public property; he had been there first, he was there by rights as a guest of the house; if anything, they were the interlopers. Besides, nobody talked secrets with a head waiter. His own long conversations with Gustavo were as open and innocent as the day; the signorina was perfectly welcome to listen to them as much as she chose.

"He had also shifted his position so that he might command the profile of the girl"

She was sitting with her chin in her hand, eyeing the flying coat-tails of Gustavo, a touch of amusement in her face. Her father was eyeing her severely.

"Constance, it is disgraceful!"

She laughed. Apparently she already knew or divined what it was that was disgraceful, but the accusation did not appear to bother her much. Mr. Wilder proceeded grumblingly.

"It's bad enough with those five deluded officers, but they walked into the trap with their eyes open and it's their own affair. But look at Gustavo; he can scarcely carry a dish without breaking it when you are watching him. And Giuseppe—that confounded *Farfalla* with its yellow sails floats back and forth in front of the terrace till I am on the point of having it scuttled as a public nuisance; and those three washer-women and the post-office clerk and the boy who brings milk, and Luigi and—every man, woman and child in the village of Valedolmo!"

"And my own dad as well?"

Mr. Wilder shook his head.

"I came here at your instigation for rest and relaxation—to get rid of nervous worries, and here I find a big new worry waiting for me that I'd never thought of having before. What if my only daughter should take it in her head to marry one of these infernally good-looking Italian officers?"

Constance reached over and patted his arm.

"Don't let it bother you, Dad; I assure you I won't do anything of the sort. I should think it my duty to learn the subjunctive mood, and that is impossible."

Gustavo came hurrying back with a tray. He arranged the glasses, the ice, the sugar, the cakes, with loving, elaborate obsequiousness. The signorina examined the ice doubtfully, then with approval.

"It's exactly right to-day, Gustavo! You got it too large the last time, you remember."

She stirred in some sugar and tasted it tentatively, her head on one side. Gustavo hung upon her expression in an agony of apprehension; one would have thought it a matter for public mourning if the lemonade were not mixed exactly right. But apparently it was right—she nodded and smiled—and Gustavo's expression assumed relief. Constance broke open a pine nut cake and settled herself for conversation.

"Haven't you any guests, Gustavo?" Her eyes glanced over the empty court-yard. "I am afraid the hotel is not having a very prosperous season."

"*Grazie*, signorina. Zer never are many in summer; it is ze dead time, but still zay come and zay go. Seven arrive last night."

"Seven! That's nice. What are they like?"

"German mountain-climbers wif nails in zer shoes. Zey have gone to Riva on ze first boat."

"That's too bad—then the hotel is empty?"

"But no! Zer is an Italian Signora wif two babies and a governess, and two English ladies and an American gentleman—"

"An American gentleman?" Her tone was languidly interested. "How long has he been here?"

"Tree—four day."

"Indeed—what is he like?"

"Nice—ver' nice." (Gustavo might well say that; his pockets were lined with the American gentleman's silver lire.) "He talk to me always. 'Gustavo,' he say, 'I am all alone; I wish to be 'mused. Come and talk Angleesh.' Yes, it is true; I have no time to finish my work; I spend whole day talking wif dis yong American gentleman. He is just a little—" He touched his head significantly.

"Really?" She raised her eyes with an air of awakened interest. "And how did he happen to come to Valedolmo?"

"He come to meet his family, his sister and his—his aunt, who are going wif him to ze Tyrollo. But zay have not arrive. Zey are in Lucerne, he says, where zer is a lion dying, and zey wish to wait until he is dead; zen zey come.—Yes, it is true; he tell me zat." Gustavo tapped his head a second time.

The signorina glanced about apprehensively.

"Is he safe, Gustavo—to be about?"

"*Si*, signorina, *sicuramente*! He is just a little simple."

Mr. Wilder chuckled.

"Where is he, Gustavo? I think I'd like to make that young man's acquaintance."

"I sink, signore, he is packing his trunk. He go away today."

"Today, Gustavo?" There was audible regret in Constance's tone. "Why is he going?"

"It is not possible for him to stand it, signorina. Valedolmo too dam slow."

"Gustavo! You mustn't say that; it is very, very bad. Nice men don't say it."

Gustavo held his ground.

"*Si*, signorina, zat yong American gentleman say it—dam slow, no *divertimento*."

"He's just about right, Gustavo," Mr. Wilder broke in. "The next time a young American gentleman blunders into the Hotel du Lac you send him around to me."

"*Si*, signore."

Gustavo rolled his eyes toward the signorina; she continued to sip her lemonade.

"I have told him yesterday an American family live at Villa Rosa; he say 'All right, I go call,' but—but I sink maybe you were not at home."

"Oh!" The signorina raised her head in apparent enlightenment. "So that was the young man? Yes, to be sure, he came, but he said he was looking for Prince Sartorio's villa. I am sorry you were away, Father, you would have enjoyed him; his English was excellent.—Did he tell you he saw me, Gustavo?"

"*Si*, signorina, he tell me."

"What did he say? Did he think I was nice?"

Gustavo looked embarrassed.

"I—I no remember, signorina."

She laughed and to his relief changed the subject.

"Those English ladies who are staying here—what do they look like? Are they young?"

Gustavo delivered himself of an inimitable gesture which suggested that the English ladies had entered the bounds of that indefinite period when the subject of age must be politely waived.

"They are tall, signorina, and of a thinness—you would not believe it possible."

"I see! And so the poor young man was bored?"

Gustavo bowed vaguely. He saw no connection.

"He was awfully good-looking," she added with a sigh. "I'm afraid I made a mistake. It would be rather fun, don't you think, Dad, to have an entertaining young American gentleman about?"

"Ump!" he grunted. "I thought you were so immensely satisfied with the officers."

"Oh, I am," she agreed with a shrug which dismissed forever the young American gentleman.

"Well, Gustavo," she added in a business-like tone, "I will tell you why we called. The doctor says the Signor Papa is getting too fat—I don't think he's too fat, do you? He seems to me just comfortably chubby; but anyway, the doctor says he needs exercise, so we're going to begin climbing mountains with nails in our shoes like the Germans. And we're going to begin tomorrow because we've got two English people at the villa who adore mountains. Do you think you can find us a guide and some donkeys? We want a nice, gentle, lady-like donkey for my aunt, and another for the English lady and a third to carry the things—and maybe me, if I get tired. Then we want a man who will twist their tails and make them go; and I am very particular about the man. I want him to be picturesque—there's no use being in Italy if you can't have things picturesque, is there, Gustavo?"

"*Si*, signorina," he bowed and resumed his attitude of strained attention.

"He must have curly hair and black eyes and white teeth and a nice smile; I should like him to wear a red sash and earrings. He must be obliging and cheerful and deferential and speak good Italian—I won't have a man who speaks only dialect. He must play the mandolin and sing Santa Lucia—I believe that's all."

"And I suppose since he is to act as guide he must know the region?" her father mildly suggested.

"Oh, no, that's immaterial; we can always ask our way."

Mr. Wilder grunted, but offered no further suggestion.

"We pay four lire a day and furnish his meals," she added munificently. "And we shall begin with the castle on Monte Baldo; then when we get very proficient we'll climb Monte Maggiore. Do you understand?"

"Ze signorina desires tree donkeys and a driver at seven o'clock to-morrow morning to climb Monte Baldo?"

"In brief, yes, but *please* remember the earrings."

* * *

Meanwhile a commotion was going on behind them. The hotel omnibus had rumbled into the court yard. A *fachino* had dragged out a leather trunk, an English hat box and a couple of valises and dumped them on the ground while he ran back for the paste pot and a pile of labels. The two under-waiters, the chamber-maid and the boy who cleaned boots had drifted into the court. It was evident that the American gentleman's departure was imminent.

The luggage was labelled and hoisted to the roof of the omnibus; they all drew up in a line with their eyes on the door; but still the young man did not come. Gustavo, over his shoulder, dispatched a waiter to hunt him up. The waiter returned breathless. The gentleman was nowhere. He had searched the entire house; there was not a trace. Gustavo sent the boot-boy flying down the arbor to search the garden; he was beginning to feel anxious. What if the gentleman in a sudden fit of melancholia had thrown himself into the lake? That would indeed be an unfortunate affair!

Constance reassured him, and at the same time she arose. It occurred to her suddenly that, since the young man was going, there was nothing to be gained by waiting, and he might think—She picked up her parasol and started for the gate, but Mr. Wilder hung back; he wanted to see the matter out.

"Father," said she reproachfully, "it's embarrassing enough for him to fee all those people without our staying and watching him do it."

"I suppose it is," he acknowledged regretfully, as he resumed his hat and umbrella and palm leaf fan.

She paused for a second in the gateway.

"*Addio*, Gustavo," she called over her shoulder. "*Don't* forget the earrings."

Gustavo bowed twice and turned back with a dazed air to direct the business in hand. The boot-boy, reappearing, shook his head. No, the gentleman was not to be found in the garden. The omnibus driver leaned from his seat and swore.

Corpo di Bacco! Did he think the boat would wait all day for the sake of one passenger? As it was, they were ten minutes late and would have to gallop every step of the way.

The turmoil of ejaculation and gesture was approaching a climax; when suddenly, who should come sauntering into the midst of it, but the young American man himself! He paused to light a cigarette, then waved his hand aloft toward his leather belongings.

"Take 'em down, Gustavo. Changed my mind; not going to-day—it's too hot."

Gustavo gasped.

"But, signore, you have paid for your ticket."

"True, Gustavo, but there is no law compelling me to use it. To tell the truth I find that I am fonder of Valedolmo than I had supposed. There is something satisfying about the peace and tranquility of the place—one doesn't realize it till the moment of parting comes. Do you think I can obtain a room for a—well, an indefinite period?"

Gustavo saw a dazzling vista of silver lire stretching into the future. With an all-inclusive gesture he placed the house, the lake, the surrounding mountains, at the disposal of the American.

"You shall have what you wish, signore. At dis season ze Hotel du Lac—"

"Is not crowded, and there are half a hundred rooms at my disposal? Very well, I will keep the one I have which commands a very attractive view of a rose-colored villa set in a grove of cypress trees."

The others had waited in a state of suspension, dumbfounded at what was going on. But as soon as the young man dipped into his pocket and fished out a handful of silver, they broke into smiles; this at least was intelligible. The silver was distributed, the luggage was hoisted down, the omnibus was dismissed. The courtyard resumed its former quiet; just the American gentleman, Gustavo and the parrot were left.

Then suddenly a frightful suspicion dawned upon Gustavo—it was more than a suspicion; it was an absolute certainty which in his excitement he had overlooked. From where had the American gentleman dropped? Not the sky, assuredly, and there was no place else possible, unless the door of the summer house. Yes, he had been in the summer house, and not sleeping either. An indefinable something about his manner informed Gustavo that he was privy to the entire conversation. Gustavo, a picture of guilty remorse, searched his memory for the words he had used. Why, oh why, had he not piled up adjectives? It was the opportunity of a lifetime and he had wantonly thrown it away.

But—to his astonished relief—the young man appeared to be bearing no malice. He appeared, on the contrary, quite unusually cheerful as he sauntered whistling, across the court and seated himself in the exact chair the signorina had occupied. He plunged his hand into his pocket suggestively—Gustavo had been the only one omitted in the distribution of silver—and drew forth a roll of bills. Having selected five crisp five-lire notes, he placed them under the sugar bowl, and watched his companion while he blew three meditative rings of smoke.

"Gustavo," he inquired, "do you suppose you could find me some nice, gentle, lady-like donkeys and a red sash and a pair of earrings?"

Gustavo's fascinated gaze had been fixed upon the sugar bowl and he had only half caught the words.

"*Scusi*, signore, I no understand."

"Just sit down, Gustavo, it makes me nervous to see you standing all the time. I can't be comfortable, you know, unless everybody else is comfortable. Now pay strict attention and see if you can grasp my meaning."

Gustavo dubiously accepted the edge of the indicated chair; he wished to humor the signore's mood, however incomprehensible that mood might be. For half an hour he listened with strained attention while the gentleman talked and toyed with the sugar bowl. Amazement, misgiving, amusement, daring, flashed in succession across his face; in the end he leaned forward with shining eyes.

"*Si, si*," he whispered after a conspiratorial glance over his shoulder, "I will do it all; you may trust to me."

The young man rose, removed the sugar bowl, and sauntered on toward the road. Gustavo pocketed the notes and gazed after him.

"*Dio mio*," he murmured as he set about gathering up the

glasses, "zese Americans!"

At the gate the young man paused to light another cigarette.

"*Addio*, Gustavo," he called over his shoulder, "*don't* forget the earrings!"

CHAPTER IV

The table was set on the terrace; breakfast was served and the company was gathered. Breakfast consisted of the usual caffè-latte, rolls and strained honey, and—since a journey was to the fore and something sustaining needed—a soft-boiled egg apiece. There were four persons present, though there should have been five. The two guests were an Englishman and his wife, whom the chances of travel had brought over night to Valedolmo.

Between them, presiding over the coffee machine, was Mr. Wilder's sister, "Miss Hazel"—never "Miss Wilder" except to the butcher and baker. It was the cross of her life, she had always affirmed, that her name was not Mary or Jane or Rebecca. "Hazel" does well enough when one is eighteen and beautiful, but when one is fifty and no longer beautiful, it is little short of absurd. But if anyone at fifty could carry such a name gracefully, it was Miss Hazel Wilder; her fifty years sat as jauntily as Constance's twenty-two. This morning she was very business-like in her short skirt, belted jacket, and green felt Alpine hat with a feather in the side. No one would mistake her for a cyclist or a golfer or a motorist or anything in the world but an Alpine climber; whatever Miss Hazel was or was not, she was always *game*.

Across from Miss Hazel sat her brother in knickerbockers, his Alpine stock at his elbow and also his fan. Since his domicile in Italy, Mr. Wilder's fan had assumed the nature of a symbol; he could no more be separated from it than St. Sebastian from his arrows or St. Laurence from his gridiron. At Mr. Wilder's elbow was the empty chair where Constance should have been—she who had insisted on six as a proper breakfast hour, and had grudgingly consented to postpone it till half-past out of deference to her sleepy-headed elders. Her father had finished his egg and hers too, before she appeared, as nonchalant and smiling as if she were out the earliest of all.

"I think you might have waited!" was her greeting from the doorway.

She advanced to the table, saluted in military fashion, dropped a kiss on her father's bald spot, and possessed herself of the empty chair. She too was clad in mountain-climbing costume, in so far as blouse and skirt and leather leggings went, but above her face there fluttered the fluffy white brim of a ruffled sun hat with a bunch of pink rosebuds set over one ear.

"I am sorry not to wear my own Alpine hat, Aunt Hazel; I look so deliciously German in it, but I simply can't afford to burn all the skin off my nose."

"You can't make us believe that," said her father. "The reason is, that Lieutenant di Ferara and Captain Coroloni are going with us today, and that this hat is more becoming than the other."

"It's one reason," Constance agreed imperturbably, "but, as I say, I don't wish to burn the skin off my nose, because that is unbecoming too. You are ungrateful, Dad," she added as she helped herself to honey with a liberal hand, "I invited them solely on your account because you like to hear them talk English. Have the donkeys come?"

"The donkeys are at the back door nibbling the buds off the rose-bushes."

"And the driver?"

"Is sitting on the kitchen doorstep drinking coffee and smiling over the top of his cup at Elizabetta. There are two of him."

"Two! I only ordered one."

"One is the official driver and the other is a boy whom he has brought along to do the work."

Constance eyed her father sharply. There was something at once guilty and triumphant about his expression.

"What is it, Dad?" she inquired sternly. "I suppose he has not got a sash and earrings."

"On the contrary, he has."

"Really? How clever of Gustavo! I hope," she added anxiously, "that he talks good Italian?"

"I don't know about his Italian, but he talks uncommonly good English."

"English!" There was reproach, disgust, disillusionment, in her tone. "Not really, father?"

"Yes, really and truly—almost as well as I do. He has lived in New York and he speaks English like a dream—real English—not the Gustavo—Lieutenant di Ferara kind. I can understand what he says."

"How simply horrible!"

"Very convenient, I should say."

"If there's anything I detest, it's an Americanized Italian—and here in Valedolmo of all places, where you have a right to demand something unique and romantic and picturesque and real. It's too bad of Gustavo! I shall never place any faith in his judgment again. You may talk English to the man if you like; I shall address him in nothing but Italian."

As they rose from the table she suggested pessimistically, "Let's go and look at the donkeys—I suppose they'll be horrid, scraggly, knock-kneed little beasts."

They turned out however to be unusually attractive, as donkeys go, and they were innocently engaged in nibbling, not rose-leaves but grass, under the tutelage of a barefoot boy. Constance patted their shaggy mouse-colored noses, made the acquaintance of the boy, whose name was Beppo, and looked about for the driver proper. He rose and bowed as she approached. His appearance was even more violently spectacular than she had ordered; Gustavo had given good measure.

Beppo and the donkeys

He wore a loose white shirt—immaculately white—with a red silk handkerchief knotted about his throat, brown corduroy knee-breeches, and a red cotton sash with the hilt of a knife conspicuously protruding. His corduroy jacket was slung carelessly across his shoulders, his hat was cocked jauntily, with a red heron feather stuck in the band; last, perfect touch of all, in his ears—at his ears rather (a close examination revealed the thread)—two golden hoops flashed in the sunlight. His skin was dark—not too dark—just a good healthy out-door tan: his brows level and heavy, his gaze candor itself. He wore a tiny suggestion of a moustache which turned up at the corners (a suspicious examination of this, might have revealed the fact that it was touched up with burnt cork); there was no doubt but that he was a handsome fellow, and his attire suggested that he knew it.

Constance clasped her hands in an ecstasy of admiration.

"Constance clasped her hands in an ecstasy of admiration"

"He's perfect!" she cried. "Where on earth did Gustavo find him? Did you ever see anything so beautiful?" she appealed to the others. "He looks like a brigand in opera bouffe."

The donkey-man reddened visibly and fumbled with his hat.

"My dear," her father warned, "he understands English."

She continued to gaze with the open admiration one would bestow upon a picture or a view or a blue-ribbon horse. The man flashed her a momentary glance from a pair of searching gray eyes, then dropped his gaze humbly to the ground.

"*Buon giorno*," he said in glib Italian.

Constance studied him more intently. There was something elusively familiar about his expression; she was sure she had seen him before.

"*Buon giorno*," she replied in Italian. "You have lived in the United States?"

"*Si*, signorina."

"What is your name?"

"I spik Angleesh," he observed.

"I don't care if you do speak English; I prefer Italian—what is your name?" She repeated the question in Italian.

"*Si*, signorina," he ventured again. An anxious look had crept to his face and he hastily turned away and commenced carrying parcels from the kitchen. Constance looked after him, puzzled and suspicious. The one insult which she could not brook was for an Italian to fail to understand her when she talked Italian. As he returned and knelt to tighten the strap of a hamper, she caught sight of the thread that held his earring. She looked a second longer, and a sudden smile of illumination flashed to her face. She suppressed it quickly and turned away.

"He seems rather slow about understanding," she remarked to the others, "but I dare say he'll do."

"The poor fellow is embarrassed," apologized her father. "His name is Tony," he added—even he had understood that much Italian.

"Was there ever an Italian who had been in America whose name was not Tony? Why couldn't he have been Angelico or Felice or Pasquale or something decently picturesque?"

"My dear," Miss Hazel objected, "I think you are hypercritical. The man is scarcely to blame for his name."

"I suppose not," she agreed, "though I should have included that in my order."

Further discussion was precluded by the appearance of a station-carriage which turned in at the gate and stopped before them. Two officers descended and saluted. In summer uniforms of white linen with gold shoulder-straps, and shining top-boots, they rivalled the donkey-man in decorativeness. Constance received them with flattering acclaim, while she noted from the corner of her eye the effect upon Tony. He had not counted upon this addition to the party, and was as scowling as she could have wished. While the officers were engaged in making their bow to the others, Constance casually reapproached the donkeys. Tony feigned immersion in the business of strapping hampers; he had no wish to be drawn into any Italian tête-à-tête. But to his relief she addressed him this time in English.

"Are these donkeys used to mountain-climbing?"

"But yes, signorina! *Sicuramente.* Zay are ver' strong, ver' good. Zat donk', signorina, he go all day and never one little stumble."

His English, she noted with amused appreciation, was an exact copy of Gustavo's; he had learned his lesson well. But she allowed not the slightest recognition of the fact to appear in her face.

"And what are their names?" she inquired.

"Dis is Fidilini, signorina, and zat one wif ze white nose is Macaroni, and zat ovver is Cristoforo Colombo."

Elizabetta appeared in the doorway with two rush-covered flasks, and Tony hurried forward to receive them. There was a complaisant set to his shoulders as he strode off, Constance noted delightedly; he was felicitating himself upon the ease with which he had fooled her. Well! She would give him cause before the day was over for other than felicitations. She stifled a laugh of prophetic triumph and sauntered over to Beppo.

"When Tony is engaged as a guide do you always go with him?"

"Not always, signorina, but Carlo has wished me to go to-day to look after the donkeys."

"And who is Carlo?"

"He is the guide who owns them."

Beppo looked momentarily guilty; the answer had slipped out before he thought.

"Oh, indeed! But if Tony is a guide why doesn't he have donkeys of his own?"

"He used to, but one unfortunately fell into the lake and got drowned and the other died of a sickness."

He put forth this preposterous statement with a glance as grave and innocent as that of a little cherub.

"Is Tony a good guide?"

"But yes, of the best!"

There was growing anxiety in Beppo's tone. He divined suspicion behind these persistent inquiries, and he knew that in case Tony were dismissed, his own munificent pay would stop.

"Do you understand any English?" she suddenly asked.

He modestly repudiated any great knowledge. "A word here, a

word there; I learn it in school."

"I see!" She paused for a moment and then inquired casually, "Have you known Tony long?"

"*Si*, signorina."

"How long?"

Beppo considered. Someone, clearly, must vouch for the man's respectability. This was not in the lesson that had been taught him, but he determined to branch out for himself.

"He is my father, signorina."

"Really! He looks young to be your father—have you any brothers and sisters, Beppo?"

"I have four brothers, signorina, and five sisters." He fell back upon the truth with relief.

"*Davvero*!"

The signorina smiled upon him, a smile of such heavenly sweetness that he instantly joined the already crowded ranks of her admirers. She drew from her pocket a handful of coppers and dropped them into his grimy little palm.

"Here, Beppo, are some soldi for the brothers and sisters. I hope that you will be good and obedient and *always* tell me the truth."

CHAPTER V

After some delay—owing to Tony's inability to balance the chafing-dish on Cristoforo Colombo's back—they filed from the gateway, an imposing cavalcade. The ladies were on foot, loftily oblivious to the fact that three empty saddles awaited their pleasure. Constance, a gesticulating officer at either hand, was vivaciously talking Italian, while Tony, trudging behind, listened with a somber light in his eye. She now and then cast a casual glance over her shoulder, and as she caught sight of his gloomy face the animation of her Italian redoubled. The situation held for her mischief-loving soul undreamed-of possibilities; and though she ostensibly occupied herself with the officers, she by no means neglected the donkey-man.

During the first few miles of the journey he earned his four francs. Twice he reshifted the pack because Constance thought it insecure (it was a disgracefully unprofessional pack; most guides would have blushed at the making of it); once he retraced their path some two hundred yards in search of a veil she thought she had dropped—it turned out that she had had it in her pocket all of the time. He chased Fidilini over half the mountainside while the others were resting, and he carried the chafing-dish for a couple of miles because it refused to adjust itself nicely to the pack. The morning ended by his being left behind with a balking donkey, while the others completed the last ascent that led to their halting-place for lunch.

It was a small plateau shaded by oak trees with a broad view below them, and a mountain stream foaming down from the rocks above. It was owing to Beppo's knowledge of the mountain paths rather than Tony's which had guided them to this agreeable spot; though no one in the party except Constance appeared to have noted the fact. Tony arrived some ten minutes after the others, hot but victorious, driving Cristoforo Colombo before him. Constance welcomed his return with an off-hand nod and set him about preparing lunch. He and Beppo served it and repacked the hampers, entirely ignored by the others of the party. Poor Tony was beginning to realize that a donkey-man lives on a desert island in so far as any companionship goes. But his moment was coming. As they were about to start on, Constance spied high above their heads where the stream burst from the rocks, a clump of starry white blossoms.

"Edelweiss!" she cried. "Oh, I must have it—it's the first I ever saw growing; I hadn't supposed we were high enough." She glanced at the officers.

The ascent was not dangerous, but it was undeniably muddy, and they both wore white; with very good cause they hesitated. And while they hesitated, the opportunity was lost. Tony sprang forward, scrambled up the precipice hand over hand, swung out across the stream by the aid of an overhanging branch and secured the flowers. It was very gracefully and easily done, and a burst of applause greeted his descent. He divided his flowers into two equal parts, and sweeping off his hat, presented them with a bow, not to Constance, but to the officers, who somewhat sulkily passed them on. She received them with a smile; for an instant her eyes met Tony's, and he fell back, rewarded.

The captain and lieutenant for the first time regarded the donkey-man, and they regarded him narrowly, red sash, earrings, stiletto and all. Constance caught the look and laughed.

"Isn't he picturesque?" she inquired in Italian. "The head-waiter at the Hotel du Lac found him for me. He has been in the United States and speaks English, which is a great convenience."

The two said nothing, but they looked at each other and shrugged.

The donkeys were requisitioned for the rest of the journey; while Tony led Miss Hazel's mount, he could watch Constance ahead on Fidilini, an officer marching at each side of her saddle.

She appeared to divide her favors with nice discrimination; it was not her fault if the two were jealous of one another. Tony could draw from that obvious fact what consolation there was in it.

"Constance ahead on Fidilini, an officer marching at each side of her saddle."

The ruined fortress, their destination, was now exactly above their heads. The last ascent boldly skirted the shoulder of the mountain, and then doubled upward in a series of serpentine coils. Below them the whole of Lake Garda was spread like a map. Mr. Wilder and the Englishman, having paused at the edge of the declivity, were endeavoring to trace the boundary line of Austria, and they called upon the officers for help. The two relinquished their post at Constance's side, while the donkeys kept on past them up the hill. The winding path was both stony and steep, and, from a donkey's standpoint, thoroughly objectionable. Fidilini was well in the lead, trotting sedately, when suddenly without the slightest warning, he chose to revolt. Whether Constance pulled the wrong rein, or whether, as she affirmed, it was merely his natural badness, in any case, he suddenly veered from the path and took a cross cut down the rocky slope below them. Donkeys are fortunately sure-footed beasts; otherwise the two would have plunged together down the sheer face of the mountain. As it was it looked ghastly enough to the four men below; they shouted to Constance to stick on, and commenced scrambling up the slope with absolutely no hope of reaching her.

It was Tony's chance a second time to show his agility—and this time to some purpose. He was a dozen yards behind and much lower down, which gave him a start. Leaping forward, he dropped over the precipice, a fall of ten feet, to a narrow ledge below. Running toward them at an angle, he succeeded in cutting off their flight. Before the frightened donkey could swerve, Tony had seized him—by the tail—and had braced himself against a boulder. It was not a dignified rescue, but at least it was effective; Fidilini came to a halt. Constance, not expecting the sudden jolt, toppled over sidewise, and Tony, being equally unprepared to receive her, the two went down together rolling over and over on the grassy slope.

"My dear, are you hurt?"

Mr. Wilder, quite pale with anxiety, came scrambling to her side. Constance sat up and laughed hysterically, while she examined a bleeding elbow.

"N—no, not dangerously—but I think perhaps Tony is."

Tony however was at least able to run, as he was again on his feet and after the donkey. Captain Coroloni and her father helped Constance to her feet while Lieutenant di Ferara recovered a side-comb and the white sun hat. They all climbed down together to the path below, none the worse for the averted tragedy. Tony rejoined them somewhat short of breath, but leading a humbled Fidilini. Constance, beyond a brief glance, said nothing; but her father, to the poor man's intense embarrassment, shook him warmly by the hand with the repeated assurance that his bravery should not go unrewarded.

They completed their journey on foot; Tony following behind, quite conscious that, if he had played the part of hero, he had done it with a lamentable lack of grace.

CHAPTER VI

Tony was stretched on the parapet that bordered the stone-paved platform of the fortress. Above him the crumbling tower rose many feet higher, below him a marvelous view stretched invitingly; but Tony had eyes neither for medieval architecture nor picturesque scenery. He lay with his coat doubled under his head for a pillow, in a frowning contemplation of the cracked stone pavement.

The four other men, after an hour or so of easy lounging under the pines at the base of the tower, had organized a fresh expedition to the summit a mile farther up. Mr. Wilder, since morning, had developed into an enthusiastic mountain-climber—regret might come with the morrow, but as yet ambition still burned high. The remainder of the party were less energetic. The three ladies were resting on rugs spread under the pines; Beppo was sleeping in the sun, his hat over his face, and the donkeys, securely tethered (Tony had attended to that) were innocently nibbling mountain herbs.

There was no obvious reason why, as he lighted a cigarette and stretched himself on the parapet, Tony should not have been the most self-satisfied guide in the world. He had not only completed the expedition in safety, but had saved the heroine's life by the way; and even if the heroine did not appear as thankful as she might, still, her father had shown due gratitude, and, what was to the point, had promised a reward. That should have been enough for any reasonable donkey-driver.

But it was distinctly not enough for Tony. He was in a fine temper as he lay on the parapet and scowled at the pavement. Nothing was turning out as he had planned. He had not counted on the officers or her predilection for Italian. He had not counted on chasing donkeys in person while she stood and looked on—Beppo was to have attended to that. He had not counted on anything quite so absurd as his heroic capture of Fidilini. Since she must let the donkey run away with her, why, in the name of all that was romantic—could it not have occurred by moonlight? Why, when he caught the beast, could it not have been by the bridle instead of the tail? And above all, why could she not have fallen into his arms, instead of on top of him?

The stage scenery was set for romance, but from the moment the curtain rose the play had persisted in being farce. However, farce or romance, it was all one to him so long as he could play leading-man; what he objected to was the minor part. The fact was clear that sash and earrings could never compete with uniform and sword and the Italian language. His mind was made up; he would withdraw tonight before he was found out, and leave Valedolmo tomorrow morning by the early boat. Miss Constance Wilder should never have the satisfaction of knowing the truth.

He was engaged in framing a dignified speech to Mr. Wilder—thanking him for his generosity, but declining to accept a reward for what had been merely a matter of duty—when his reflections were cut short by the sound of footsteps on the stairs. They were by no means noiseless footsteps; there were good strong nails all over the bottom of Constance's shoes. The next moment she appeared in the doorway. Her eyes were centered on the view; she looked entirely over Tony. It was not until he rose to his feet that she realized his presence with a start.

"Dear me, is that you, Tony? You frightened me! Don't get up; I know you must be tired." This with a sweetly solicitous smile.

Tony smiled too and resumed his seat; it was the first time since morning that she had condescended to consider his feelings. She sauntered over to the opposite side and stood with her back to him examining the view. Tony turned his back and affected to be engaged with the view in the other direction; he too could play at indifference.

Constance finished with her view first, and crossing over, she seated herself in the deep embrasure of a window close beside Tony's parapet. He rose again at her approach, but there was no eagerness in the motion; it was merely the necessary deference of a donkey-driver toward his employer.

"She seated herself in the deep embrasure of a window close beside Tony's parapet"

"Oh, sit down," she insisted, "I want to talk to you."

He opened his eyes with a show of surprise; his hurt feelings insisted that all the advances should be on her part. Constance seemed in no hurry to begin; she removed her hat, pushed back her hair, and sat playing with the bunch of edelweiss which was stuck in among the roses—flattening the petals, rearranging the flowers with careful fingers; a touch, it seemed to Tony's suddenly clamoring senses, that was almost a caress. Then she looked up quickly and caught his gaze. She leaned forward with a laugh.

"Tony," she said, "do you spik any language besides Angleesh?"

He triumphantly concealed all sign of emotion.

"*Si*, signorina, I spik my own language."

"Would you mind my asking what that language is?"

He indulged in a moment's deliberation. Italian was clearly out of the question, and French she doubtless knew better than he—he deplored this polyglot education girls were receiving nowadays.

He had it! He would be Hungarian. His sole fellow guest in the hotel at Verona the week before had been a Hungarian nobleman, who had informed him that the Magyar language was one of the most difficult on the face of the globe. There was at least little likelihood that she was acquainted with that.

"My own language, signorina, is Magyar."

"Magyar?" She was clearly taken by surprise.

"*Si*, signorina, I am Hungarian; I was born in Budapest." He met her wide-opened eyes with a look of innocent candor.

"Really!" She beamed upon him delightedly; he was playing up even better than she had hoped. "But if you are Hungarian, what are you doing here in Italy, and how does it happen that your name is Antonio?"

"My movver was Italian. She name me Antonio after ze blessed Saint Anthony of Padua. If you lose anysing, signorina, and you say a prayer to Saint Anthony every day for nine days, on ze morning of ze tenth you will find it again."

"That is very interesting," she said politely. "How do you come to know English so well, Tony?"

"We go live in Amerik' when I li'l boy."

"And you never learned Italian? I should think your mother would have taught it to you."

He imitated Beppo's gesture.

"A word here, a word there. We spik Magyar at home."

"Talk a little Magyar, Tony. I should like to hear it."

"What shall I say, signorina?"

"Oh, say anything you please."

He affected to hesitate while he rehearsed the scraps of language at his command. Latin—French—German—none of them any good—but, thank goodness, he had elected Anglo-Saxon in college; and thank goodness again the professor had made them learn passages by heart. He glanced up with an air of flattered diffidence and rendered, in a conversational inflection, an excerpt from the Anglo-Saxon Bible.

"*Ealle gesceafta, heofonas and englas, sunnan and monan, steorran and eorthan, hè gesceop and geworhte on six dagum.*"

"It is a very beautiful language. Say some more."

He replied with glib promptness, with a passage from Beowulf.

"*Hie dygel lond warigeath, wulfhleothu, windige naessas.*"

"What does that mean?"

Tony looked embarrassed.

"I don't believe you know!"

"It means—*scusi*, signorina, I no like to say."

"You don't know."

"It means—you make me say, signorina,—'I sink you ver' beautiful like ze angels in Paradise.'"

"Indeed! A donkey-driver, Tony, should not say anything like that."

"But it is true."

"The more reason you should not say it."

"You asked me, signorina; I could not tell you a lie."

The signorina smiled slightly and looked away at the view; Tony seized the opportunity to look sidewise at her. She turned back and caught him; he dropped his eyes humbly to the floor.

"Does Beppo speak Magyar?" she inquired.

"Beppo?" There was wonder in his tone at the turn her questions were taking. "I sink not, signorina."

"That must be very inconvenient. Why don't you teach it to him?"

"*Si*, signorina." He was plainly nonplussed.

"Yes, he says that you are his father and I should think—"

"His father?" Tony appeared momentarily startled; then he laughed. "He did not mean his real father; he mean—how you say—his god-father. I give to him his name when he get christened."

"Oh, I see!"

Her next question was also a surprise.

"Tony," she inquired with startling suddenness, "why do you wear earrings?"

He reddened slightly.

"Because—because—der's a girl I like ver' moch, signorina; she sink earrings look nice. I wear zem for her."

"Oh!—But why do you fasten them on with thread?"

"Because I no wear zem always. In Italia, yes; in Amerik' no. When I marry dis girl and go back home, zen I do as I please, now I haf to do as she please."

"H'm—" said Constance, ruminatingly. "Where does this girl live, Tony?"

"In Valedolmo, signorina."

"What does she look like?"

"She look like—" His eyes searched the landscape and came back to her face. "Oh, ver' beautiful, signorina. She have hair brown and gold, and eyes—yes, eyes! Zay are sometimes black, signorina, and sometimes gray. Her laugh, it sounds like the song of a nightingale." He clasped his hands and rolled his eyes in a fine imitation of Gustavo. "She is beautiful, signorina, beautiful as ze angels in Paradise!"

"There seem to be a good many people beautiful as the angels in Paradise."

"She is most beautiful of all."

"What is her name?"

"Costantina." He said it softly, his eyes on her face.

"Ah," Constance rose and turned away with a shrug. Her manner suggested that he had gone too far.

"She wash clothes at ze Hotel du Lac," he called after her.

Constance paused and glanced over her shoulder with a laugh.

"Tony," she said, "the quality which I admire most in a donkey-driver, besides truthfulness and picturesqueness, is imagination."

CHAPTER VII

On the homeward journey Tony again trudged behind while the officers held their post at Constance's side. But Tony's spirits were still singing from the little encounter on the castle platform, and in spite of the animated Italian which floated back, he was determined to look at the sunny side of the adventure. It was Mr. Wilder who unconsciously supplied him with a second opportunity for conversation. He and the Englishman, being deep in a discussion involving statistics of the Italian army budget, called on the two officers to set them straight. Tony, at their order, took his place beside the saddle; Constance was not to be abandoned again to Fidilini's caprice. Miss Hazel and the Englishwoman were ambling on ahead in as matter-of-fact a fashion as if that were their usual mode of travel. Their donkeys were of a sedater turn of mind than Fidilini—a fact for which Tony offered thanks.

They were by this time well over the worst part of the mountain and the brief Italian twilight was already fading. Tony, with a sharp eye on the path ahead and a ready hand for the bridle, was attending strictly to the duties of a well-trained donkey-man. It was Constance again who opened the conversation.

"Ah, Tony?"

"*Si*, signorina?"

"Did you ever read any Angleesh books—or do you do most of your reading in Magyar?"

"I haf read one, two, Angleesh books."

"Did you ever read—er—'The Lightning Conductor' for example?"

"No, signorina; I haf never read heem."

"I think it would interest you. It's about a man who pretends he's a chauffeur in order to—to— There are any number of books with the same motive; 'She Stoops to Conquer,' 'Two Gentlemen of Verona,' 'Lalla Rookh,' 'Monsieur Beaucaire'—Oh, dozens of them! It's an old plot; it doesn't require the slightest originality to think of it."

"*Si*, signorina? Sank you." Tony's tone was exactly like Gustavo's when he has failed to get the point, but feels that a comment is necessary.

Constance laughed and allowed a silence to follow, while Tony redirected his attention to Fidilini's movements. His "Yip! Yip!" was an exact imitation, though in a deeper guttural, of Beppo's cries before them. It would have taken a close observer to suspect that he had not been bred to the calling.

"You have not always been a donkey-driver?" she inquired after an interval of amused scrutiny.

"Not always, signorina."

"What did you do in New York?"

"I play hand-organ, signorina."

Tony removed his hand from the bridle and ground "Yankee Doodle" from an imaginary instrument.

"I make musica, signorina, wif—wif—how you say, monk, monka? His name Vittorio Emanuele. Ver' nice monk—simpatica affezionata."

"You've never been an actor?"

"An actor? No, signorina."

"You should try it; I fancy you might have some talent in that direction."

"*Si*, signorina. Sank you."

She let the conversation drop, and Tony, after an interval of silence, fell to humming Santa Lucia in a very presentable baritone. The tune, Constance noted, was true enough, but the words were far astray.

"That's a very pretty song, Tony, but you don't appear to know it."

"I no understand Italian, signorina. I just learn ze tune because

Costantina like it."

"You do everything that Costantina wishes?"

"Everysing! But if you could see her you would not wonder. She has hair brown and gold, and her eyes, signorina, are sometimes gray and sometimes black, and her laugh sounds like—"

"Oh, yes, I know; you told me all that before."

"When she goes out to work in ze morning, signorina, wif the sunlight shining on her hair, and a smile on her lips, and a basket of clothes on her head—Ah, *zen* she is beautiful!"

"When are you going to be married?"

"I do not know, signorina. I have not asked her yet."

"Then how do you know she wishes to marry you?"

"I do not know; I just hope."

He rolled his eyes toward the moon which was rising above the mountains on the other side of the lake, and with a deep sigh he fell back into Santa Lucia.

Constance leaned forward and scanned his face.

"Tony! Tell me your name." There was an undertone of meaning, a note of persuasion in her voice.

"Antonio, signorina."

She shook her head with a show of impatience.

"Your real name—your last name."

"Yamhankeesh."

"Oh!" she laughed. "Antonio Yamhankeesh doesn't seem to me a very musical combination; I don't think I ever heard anything like it before."

"It suits me, signorina." His tone carried a suggestion of wounded dignity. "Yamhankeesh has a ver' beautiful meaning in my language—'He who dares not, wins not'."

"And that is your motto?"

"*Si*, signorina."

"A very dangerous motto, Tony; it will some day get you into trouble."

They had reached the base of the mountain and their path now broadened into the semblance of a road which wound through the fields, between fragrant hedgerows, under towering chestnut trees. All about them was the fragrance of the dewy, flower-scented summer night, the flash of fireflies, the chirp of crickets, occasionally the note of a nightingale. Before them out of a cluster of cypresses, rose the square graceful outline of the village campanile.

Constance looked about with a pleased, contented sigh.

"Isn't Italy beautiful, Tony?"

"Yes, signorina, but I like America better."

"We have no cypresses and ruins and nightingales in America, Tony. We have a moon sometimes, but not that moon."

They passed from the moonlight into the shade of some overhanging chestnut trees. Fidilini stumbled suddenly over a break in the path and Tony pulled him up sharply. His hand on the bridle rested for an instant over hers.

"Italy is beautiful—to make love in," he whispered.

She drew her hand away abruptly, and they passed out into the moonlight again. Ahead of them where the road branched into the highway, the others were waiting for Constance to catch up, the two officers looking back with an eager air of expectation. Tony glanced ahead and added with a quick frown.

"But perhaps I do not need to tell you that—you may know it already?"

"You are impertinent, Tony."

She pulled the donkey into a trot that left him behind.

The highway was broad and they proceeded in a group, the conversation general and in English, Tony quite naturally having no part in it. But at the corners where the road to the village and the road to the villa separated, Fidilini obligingly turned stubborn again. His mind bent upon rest and supper, he insisted upon going to the village; the harder Constance pulled on the left rein, the more fixed was his determination to turn to the right.

"Help! I'm being run away with again," she called over her shoulder as the donkey's pace quickened into a trot.

Tony, awakening to his duty, started in pursuit, while the others laughingly shouted directions. He did not run as determinedly as he might and they had covered considerable ground before he overtook them. He turned Fidilini's head and they started back—at a walk.

"Signorina," said Tony, "may I ask a question, a little impertinent?"

"No, certainly not."

Silence.

"Ah, Tony?" she asked presently.

"*Si*, signorina?"

"What is it you want to ask?"

"Are you going to marry that Italian lieutenant—or perhaps the captain?"

"That *is* impertinent."

"Are you?"

"You forget yourself, Tony. It is not your place to ask such a question."

"*Si*, signorina; it is my place. If it is true I cannot be your donkey-man any longer."

"No, it is not true, but that is no concern of yours."

"Are you going on another trip Friday—to Monte Maggiore?"

"Yes."

"May I come with you?"

His tone implied more than his words. She hesitated a moment, then shrugged indifferently.

"Just as you please, Tony. If you don't wish to work for us any more I dare say we can find another man."

"It is as you please, signorina. If you wish it, I come, if you do not wish it, I go."

She made no answer. They joined the others and the party proceeded to the villa gates.

Lieutenant di Ferara helped Constance dismount, while Captain Coroloni, with none too good a grace, held the donkey. A careful observer would have fancied that the lieutenant was ahead, and that both he and the captain knew it. Tony untied the bundles, dumped them on the kitchen floor, and waited respectfully, hat in hand, while Mr. Wilder searched his pockets for change. He counted out four lire and added a note. Tony pocketed the lire and returned the note, while Mr. Wilder stared his astonishment.

"Good-bye, Tony," Constance smiled as he turned away.

"Good-bye, signorina." There was a note of finality in his voice.

"Well!" Mr. Wilder ejaculated. "That is the first—" "Italian" he started to say, but he caught the word before it was out "—donkey-driver I ever saw refuse money."

Lieutenant di Ferara raised his shoulders.

"*Machè*! The fellow is too honest; you do well to watch him." There was a world of disgust in his tone.

Constance glanced after the retreating figure and laughed.

"Tony!" she called.

He kept on; she raised her voice.

"Mr. Yamhankeesh."

He paused.

"You call, signorina?"

"Be sure and be here by half past six on Friday morning; we must start early."

"Sank you, signorina. Good-night."

"Good-night, Tony."

CHAPTER VIII

The Hotel du Lac may be approached in two ways. The ordinary, obvious way, which incoming tourists of necessity choose, is by the highroad and the gate. But the romantic way is by water. One sees only the garden then and the garden is the distinguished feature of the place; it was planned long before the hotel was built to adorn a marquis's pleasure house. There are grottos, arbors, fountains, a winding stream; and, stretching the length of the water front, a deep cool grove of interlaced plane trees. At the end of the grove, half a dozen broad stone steps dip down to a tiny harbor which is carpeted on the surface with lily pads. The steps are worn by the lapping waves of fifty years, and are grown over with slippery, slimy water weeds.

The world was just stirring from its afternoon siesta, when the *Farfalla* dropped her yellow sails and floated into the shady little harbor. Giuseppe prodded and pushed along the fern-grown banks until the keel jolted against the water steps. He sprang ashore and steadied the boat while Constance alighted. She slipped on the mossy step—almost went under—and righted herself with a laugh that rang gaily through the grove.

She came up the steps still smiling, shook out her fluffy pink skirts, straightened her rose-trimmed hat, and glanced reconnoiteringly about the grove. One might reasonably expect, attacking the hotel as it were from the flank, to capture unawares any stray guest. But aside from a chaffinch or so and a brown-and-white spotted calf tied to a tree, the grove was empty—blatantly empty. There was a shade of disappointment in Constance's glance. One naturally does not like to waste one's best embroidered gown on a spotted calf.

Then her eye suddenly brightened as it lighted on a vivid

splash of yellow under a tree. She crossed over and picked it up—a paper covered French novel; the title was *Bijou*, the author was Gyp. She turned to the first page. Any reasonably careful person might be expected to write his name in the front of a book—particularly a French book—before abandoning it to the mercies of a foreign hotel. But the several fly leaves were immaculately innocent of all sign of ownership.

So intent was she upon this examination, that she did not hear footsteps approaching down the long arbor that led from the house; so intent was the young man upon a frowning scrutiny of the path before him, that he did not see Constance until he had passed from the arbor into the grove. Then simultaneously they raised their heads and looked at each other. For a startled second they stared—rather guiltily—both with the air of having been caught. Constance recovered her poise first; she nodded—a nod which contained not the slightest hint of recognition—and laughed.

"Oh!" she said. "I suppose this is your book? And I am afraid you have caught me red-handed. You must excuse me for looking at it, but usually at this season only German Alpine-climbers stop at the Hotel du Lac, and I was surprised you know to find that German Alpine-climbers did anything so frivolous as reading Gyp."

The man bowed with a gesture which made her free of the book, but he continued his silence. Constance glanced at him again, and this time she allowed a flash of recognition to appear in her face.

"The man bowed with a gesture which made her free of the book"

"Oh!" she re-exclaimed with a note of interested politeness, "you are the young man who stumbled into Villa Rosa last Monday looking for the garden of the prince?"

He bowed a second time, an answering flash appearing in his face.

"And you are the young woman who was sitting on the wall beside a row of—of—"

"Stockings?" She nodded. "I trust you found the prince's garden without difficulty?"

"Yes, thank you. Your directions were very explicit."

A slight pause followed, the young man waiting deferentially for her to take the lead.

"You find Valedolmo interesting?" she inquired.

"Interesting!" His tone was enthusiastic. "Aside from the prince's garden which contains a cedar of Lebanon and an India rubber plant from South America, there is the Luini in the chapel of San Bartolomeo, and the statue of Garibaldi in the piazza. And then—" he waved his hand toward the lake, "there is always the view."

"Yes," she agreed, "one can always look at the view."

Her eyes wandered to the lake, and across the lake to Monte Maggiore with clouds drifting about its peak. And while she obligingly studied the mountain, he studied the effect of the pink gown and the rose-bud hat. She turned back suddenly and caught him; it was a disconcerting habit of Constance's. He politely looked away and she—with frank interest—studied him. He was bareheaded and dressed in white flannels; they were very becoming, she noted critically, and yet—they needed just a touch of color; a red sash, for example, and earrings.

"The guests of the Hotel du Lac," she remarked, "have a beautiful garden of their own. Just the mere pleasure of strolling about in it ought to keep them contented with Valedolmo."

"Not necessarily," he objected. "Think of the garden of Eden—the most beautiful garden there has ever been if report speaks true—and yet the mere pleasure of strolling about didn't keep Adam contented. One gets lonely you know."

"Are you the only guest?"

"Oh, no, there are four of us, but we're not very companionable; there's such a discrepancy in languages."

"And you don't speak Italian?"

He shook his head.

"Only English and—" he glanced at the book in her hand—"French indifferently well."

"I saw someone the other day who spoke Magyar—that is a beautiful language."

"Yes?" he returned with polite indifference. "I don't remember ever to have heard it."

She laughed and glanced about. Her eyes lighted on the arbor hung with grape-vines and wistaria, where, far at the other end, Gustavo's figure was visible lounging in the yellow stucco doorway. The sight appeared to recall an errand to her mind. She glanced down at a pink wicker-basket which hung on her arm, and gathered up her skirts with a movement of departure.

The young man hastily picked up the conversation.

"It *is* a jolly old garden," he affirmed. "And there's something pathetic about its appearing on souvenir post-cards as a mere adjunct to a blue and yellow hotel."

She nodded sympathetically.

"Built for romance and abandoned to tourists—German tourists at that!"

"Oh, not entirely—we've a Russian countess just now."

"A Russian countess?" Constance turned toward him with an air of reawakened interest. "Is she as young and beautiful and fascinating and wicked as they always are in novels?"

"Oh, dear no! Seventy, if she's a day. A nice grandmotherly old soul who smokes cigarettes."

"Ah!" Constance smiled; there was even a trace of relief in her manner as she nodded to the young man and turned away. His face reflected his disappointment; he plainly wished to detain her, but could think of no expedient. The spotted calf came to his rescue. The calf had been watching them from the first, very much interested in the visitor; and now as she approached his tree, he stretched out his neck as far as the tether permitted and sniffed insistently. She paused and patted him on the head. The calf acknowledged the caress with a grateful *moo*; there was a plaintive light in his liquid eyes.

"Poor thing—he's lonely!" She turned to the young man and spoke with an accent of reproach. "The four guests of the Hotel du Lac don't show him enough attention."

The young man shrugged.

"We're tired of calves. It's only a matter of a day or so before he'll be breaded and fried and served Milanese fashion with a sauce of tomato and garlic."

Constance shook her head sympathetically; though whether her sympathy was for the calf or the partakers of *table d'hote*, was not quite clear.

"I know," she agreed. "I've been a guest at the Hotel du Lac myself—it's a tragedy to be born a calf in Italy!"

She nodded and turned; it was evident this time that she was really going. He took a hasty step forward.

"Oh, I say, please don't go! Stay and talk to me—just a little while. That calf isn't half so lonely as I am."

"I should like to, but really I mustn't. Elizabetta is waiting for me to bring her some eggs. We are planning a trip up the Maggiore tomorrow, and we have to have a cake to take with us. Elizabetta made one this morning but she forgot to put in the baking powder. Italian cooks are not used to making cakes; they are much better at—" her eyes fell on the calf—"veal and such things."

He folded his arms with an air of desperation.

"I'm an American—one of your own countrymen; if you had a grain of charity in your nature you would let the cake go."

She shook her head relentlessly.

"Five days at Valedolmo! You would not believe the straits I've been driven to in search of amusement."

"Yes?" There was a touch of curiosity in her tone. "What for example?"

"I am teaching Gustavo how to play tennis."

"Oh!" she said. "How does he do?"

"Broken three windows and a flower pot and lost four balls."

She laughed and turned away; and then as an idea occurred to her, she turned back and fixed her eyes sympathetically on his face.

"I suppose Valedolmo *is* stupid for a man; but why don't you try mountain climbing? Everybody finds that diverting. There's a guide here who speaks English—really comprehensible English. He's engaged for tomorrow, but after that I dare say he'll be free. Gustavo can tell you about him."

She nodded and smiled and turned down the arbor.

The young man stood where she left him, with folded arms, watching her pink gown as it receded down the long sun-flecked alley hung with purple and green. He waited until it had been swallowed up in the yellow doorway; then he fetched a deep breath and strolled to the water-wall. After a few moments' prophetic contemplation of the mountain across the lake, he threw back his head with a quick amused laugh, and got out a cigarette and lighted it.

CHAPTER IX

As Constance emerged at the other end of the arbor, Gustavo, who had been nodding on the bench beside the door, sprang to his feet, consternation in his attitude.

"Signorina!" he stammered. "You come from ze garden?"

She nodded in her usual off-hand manner and handed him the basket.

"Eggs, Gustavo—two dozen if you can spare them. I am sorry always to be wanting so many, but—" she sighed, "eggs are so breakable!"

Gustavo rolled his eyes to heaven in silent thanksgiving. She had not, it was evident, run across the American, and the cat was still safely in the bag; but how much longer it could be kept there, the saints alone knew. He was feeling—very properly—guilty in regard to this latest escapade; but what can a defenceless waiter do in the hands of an impetuous young American whose pockets are stuffed with silver lire and five-franc notes?

"Two dozen? Certainly, signorina. *Subitissimo*!" He took the basket and hurried to the kitchen.

Constance occupied the interval with the polyglot parrot of the courtyard. The parrot, since she had last conversed with him, had acquired several new expressions in the English tongue. As Gustavo reappeared with the eggs, she confronted him sternly.

"Have you been teaching this bird English? I am surprised!"

"No, signorina. It was—it was—" Gustavo mopped his brow. "He jus' pick it up."

"I'm sorry that the Hotel du Lac has *guests* that use such language; it's very shocking."

"*Si*, signorina."

"By the way, Gustavo, how does it happen that that young

American man who left last week is still here?"

Gustavo nearly dropped the eggs.

"I just saw him in the garden with a book—I am sure it was the same young man. What is he doing all this time in Valedolmo?"

Gustavo's eyes roved wildly until they lighted on the tennis court.

"He—he stay, signorina, to play lawn tennis wif me, but he go tomorrow."

"Oh, he is going tomorrow?—What's his name, Gustavo?"

She put the question indifferently while she stooped to pet a tortoise-shell cat that was curled asleep on the bench.

"His name?" Gustavo's face cleared. "I get ze raygeester; you read heem yourself."

He darted into the bureau and returned with a black book.

"*Ecco*, signorina!" spreading it on the table before her.

His alacrity should have aroused her suspicions; but she was too intent on the matter in hand. She turned the pages and paused at the week's entries; Rudolph Ziegelmann und Frau, Berlin; and just beneath, in bold black letters that stretched from margin to margin, Abraham Lincoln, U. S. A.

"She turned the pages and paused at the week's entries."

Gustavo hovered above anxiously watching her face; he had been told that this would make everything right, that Abraham Lincoln was an exceedingly respectable name. Constance's expression did not change. She looked at the writing for fully three minutes, then she opened her purse and looked inside. She laid the money for the eggs in a pile on the table, and took out an extra lira which she held in her hand.

"Gustavo," she asked, "do you think that you *could* tell me the truth?"

"Signorina!" he said reproachfully.

"How did that name get there?"

"He write it heemself!"

"Yes, I dare say he did—but it doesn't happen to be his name. Oh, I'm not blind; I can see plainly enough that he has scratched out his own name underneath."

Gustavo leaned forward and affected to examine the page. "It was a li'l' blot, signorina; he scratch heem out."

"Gustavo!" Her tone was despairing. "Are you incapable of telling the truth? That young man's name is no more Abraham Lincoln than Victor Emmanuel II. When did he write that and why?"

Gustavo's eyes were on the lira; he broke down and told the truth.

"Yesterday night, signorina. He say, 'ze next time zat Signorina Americana who is beautiful as ze angels come to zis hotel she look in ze raygeester, an' I haf it feex ready'."

"Oh, he said that, did he?"

"*Si*, signorina."

"And his real name that comes on his letters?"

"Jayreem Ailyar, signorina.

"Say it again, Gustavo." She cocked her head.

He gathered himself together for a supreme effort. He rolled his r's; he shouted until the courtyard reverberated.

"Meestair-r Jay-r-reem Ailyar-r!"

Constance shook her head.

"Sounds like Hungarian—at least the way you pronounce it. But anyway it's of no consequence; I merely asked out of idle curiosity. And Gustavo—" She still held the lira—"if he asks you if I looked in this register, what are you going to say?"

"I say, 'no, Meestair Ailyar, she stay all ze time in ze courtyard talking wif ze parrot, and she was ver' moch shocked at his Angleesh'."

"Ah!" Constance smiled and laid the lira on the table. "Gustavo," she said, "I hope, for the sake of your immortal soul, that you go often to confession."

The eggs were not heavy, but Gustavo insisted upon carrying them; he was determined to see her safely aboard the *Farfalla*, with no further accidents possible. That she had not identified the young man of the garden with the donkey-driver of yesterday was clear—though how such blindness was possible, was not clear.

Probably she had only caught a glimpse of his back at a distance; in any case he thanked a merciful Providence and decided to risk no further chance. As they neared the end of the arbor, Gustavo was talking—shouting fairly; their approach was heralded.

They turned into the grove. To Gustavo's horror the most conspicuous object in it was this same reckless young man, seated on the water-wall nonchalantly smoking a cigarette. The young man rose and bowed; Constance nodded carelessly, while Gustavo behind her back made frantic signs for him to flee, to escape while still there was time. The young man telegraphed back by the same sign language that there was no danger; she didn't suspect the truth. And to Gustavo's amazement, he fell in beside them and strolled over to the water steps. His recklessness was catching; Gustavo suddenly determined upon a bold stroke himself.

"Signorina," he asked, "zat man I send, zat donk' driver—you like heem?"

"Tony?" Her manner was indifferent. "Oh, he does well enough; he seems honest and truthful, though a little stupid."

Gustavo and the young man exchanged glances.

"And Gustavo," she turned to him with a sweetly serious air that admitted no manner of doubt but that she was in earnest. "I told this young man that in case he cared to do any mountain climbing, you would find him the same guide. It would be very useful for him to have one who speaks English."

Gustavo bowed in mute acquiescence. He could find no adequate words for the situation.

The boat drew alongside and Constance stepped in, but she did not sit down. Her attention was attracted by two washer-women who had come clattering on to the little rustic bridge that spanned the stream above the water steps. The women, their baskets of linen on their heads, had paused to watch the embarkation.

"Ah, Gustavo," Constance asked over her shoulder, "is there a washer-woman here at the Hotel du Lac named Costantina?"

"*Si*, signorina, zat is Costantina standing on ze bridge wif ze yellow handkerchief on her head."

Constance looked at Costantina, and nodded and smiled. Then she laughed out loud, a beautiful rippling, joyous laugh that rang through the grove and silenced the chaffinches.

Perhaps once upon a time Costantina was beautiful—beautiful as the angels—but if so, it was long, long ago. Now she was old and fat with a hawk nose and a double chin and one tooth left in the middle of the front. But if she were not beautiful, she was at least a cheerful old soul, and, though she could not possibly know the reason, she echoed the signorina's laugh until she nearly shook the clean clothes into the water.

Constance settled herself among the cushions and glanced back toward the terrace.

"Good afternoon," she nodded politely to the young man.

He bowed with his hand on his heart.

"*Addio*, Gustavo."

He bowed until his napkin swept the ground.

"*Addio*, Costantina," she waved her hand toward her namesake.

The washer-woman laughed again and her earrings flashed in the sunlight.

Giuseppe raised the yellow sail; they caught the breeze, and the *Farfalla* floated away.

CHAPTER X

Half past six on Friday morning and Constance appeared on the terrace; Constance in fluffy, billowy, lacy white with a spray of oleander in her belt—the last costume in the world in which one would start on a mountain climb. She cast a glance in passing toward the gateway and the stretch of road visible beyond, but both were empty, and seating herself on the parapet, she turned her attention to the lake. The breeze that blew from the farther shore brought fresh Alpine odors of flowers and pine trees. Constance sniffed it eagerly as she gazed across toward the purple outline of Monte Maggiore. The serenity of her smile gradually gave place to doubt; she turned and glanced back toward the house, visibly changing her mind.

But before the change was finished, the quiet of the morning was broken by a clatter of tiny scrambling obstinate hoofs and a series of ejaculations, both Latin and English. She glanced toward the gate where Fidilini was visible, plainly determined not to come in. Constance laughed expectantly and turned back to the water, her eyes intent on the fishing-smacks that were putting out from the little *marino*. The sounds of coercion increased; a command floated down the driveway in the English tongue. It sounded like:

"You twist his tail, Beppo, while I pull."

Apparently it was understood in spite of Beppo's slight knowledge of the language. An eloquent silence followed; then an outraged grunt on the part of Fidilini, and the cavalcade advanced with a rush to the kitchen door. Tony left Beppo and the donkeys, and crossed the terrace alone. His bow swept the ground in the deferential manner of Gustavo, but his glance was far bolder than a donkey-driver's should have been. She noted the fact and tossed him a nod of marked condescension. A silence followed during which Constance studied the lake; when she turned back, she found Tony arranging a spray of oleander that had dropped from her belt in the band of his hat. She viewed this performance in silent disfavor. Having finished to his satisfaction, he tossed the hat aside and seated himself on the balustrade. Her frown became visible. Tony sprang to his feet with an air of anxiety.

"*Scusi*, signorina. I have not meant to be presumptious. Perhaps it is not fitting that anyone below the rank of lieutenant should sit in your presence?"

"It will not be very long, Tony, before you are discharged for impertinence."

"Ah, signorina, do not say that! If it is your wish I will kneel when I address you. My family, signorina, are poor; they need the four francs which you so munificently pay."

"You told me that you were an orphan; that you had no family."

"I mean the family which I hope to have. Costantina has extravagant tastes and coral earrings cost two-fifty a pair."

Constance laughed and assumed a more lenient air. She made a slight gesture which might be interpreted as an invitation to sit down; and Tony accepted it.

"By the way, Tony, how do you talk to Costantina, since she speaks no English and you no Italian?"

"We have no need of either Italian or English; the language of love, signorina, is universal."

"Oh!" she laughed again. "I was at the Hotel du Lac yesterday; I saw Costantina."

"You saw Costantina!—Ah, signorina, is she not beautiful? Ze mos' beautiful in all ze world? But ver' unkind signorina. Yes, she laugh at me; she smile at ozzer men, at soldiers wif uniforms." He sighed profoundly. "But I love her just ze same, always from ze first moment I see her. It was washday, signorina, by ze lac. I climb over ze wall and talk wif her, but she make fun of me—ver' unkind. I go away ver' sad. No use, I say, she like dose soldiers best. But I see her again; I hear her laugh—it sound like angels singing—I say, no, I can not go away; I stay here and make her love me. Yes, I do everysing she ask—but everysing! I wear earrings; I make myself into a fool just to please zat Costantina."

He leaned forward and looked into her eyes. A slow red flush crept over Constance's face and she turned her head away and looked across the water.

Mr. Wilder, in full Alpine regalia, stepped out upon the terrace and viewed the beauty of the morning with a prophetic eye. Miss Hazel followed in his wake; she wore a lavender dimity. And suddenly it occurred to Tony's slow moving masculine perception that neither lavender dimity nor white muslin were fabrics fit for mountain climbing.

Constance slipped down from her parapet and hurried to meet them.

"Good-morning, Aunt Hazel. Morning, Dad! You look beautiful! There's nothing so becoming to a man as knickerbockers—especially if he's a little stout.—You're late," she added with a touch of severity. "Breakfast has been waiting half an hour and Tony fifteen minutes."

She turned back toward the donkey-man who was standing, hat in hand, respectfully waiting orders. "Oh, Tony, I forgot to tell you; we shall not need Beppo and the donkeys to-day. You and my father are going alone."

"You no want to climb Monte Maggiore—ver' beautiful mountain." There was disappointment, reproach, rebellion in his tone.

"We have made inquiries and my aunt thinks it too long a trip. Without the donkeys you can cross by boat, and that cuts off three miles."

"As you please, signorina." He turned away.

Constance looked after him with a shade of remorse. When this plan of sending her father and Tony alone had occurred to her as she sailed homeward yesterday from the Hotel du Lac, it had seemed a humorous and fitting retribution. The young man had been just a trifle too sure of her interest; the episode of the hotel register must not go unpunished. But—it was a beautiful morning, a long empty day stretched before her, and Monte Maggiore looked alluring; there was no pursuit, for the moment, which she enjoyed as much as donkey-riding. Oh yes, she was spiting herself as well as Tony; but considering the circumstances the sacrifice seemed necessary.

When the *Farfalla* drifted up ready to take the mountain-climbers, Miss Hazel suggested (Constance possessed to a large degree the diplomatic faculty of making other people propose what she herself had decided on) that she and her niece cross with them. Tony was sulky and Constance could not forego the pleasure of baiting him further.

They put in at the village, on their way, for the morning mail; Mr. Wilder wished his paper, even at the risk of not beginning the ascent before the sun was high. Giuseppe brought back from the post, among other matters, a letter for Constance. The address was in a dashing, angular hand that pretty thoroughly covered the envelope. Had she not been so intent on the writing herself, she would have noted Tony's astonished stare as he passed it to her.

"Why!" she exclaimed, "here's a letter from Nannie Hilliard, postmarked Lucerne."

"Lucerne!" Miss Hazel echoed her surprise. "I thought they were to be in England for the summer?"

"They were—the last I heard." Constance ripped the letter open and read it aloud.

"Constance ripped the letter open and read it aloud."

"Dear Constance: You'll doubtless be surprised to hear from us in Switzerland instead of in England, and to learn further, that in the course of a week, we shall arrive at Valedolmo en route for the Dolomites. Jerry Junior at the last moment decided to come with us, and you know what a *man* is when it comes to European travel. Instead of taking two months comfortably to England, as Aunt Kate and I had planned, we did the whole of the British Isles in ten days, and Holland and France at the same breathless rate.

"Jerry says he holds the record for the Louvre; he struck a six-mile pace at the entrance, and by looking neither to the right nor the left he did the whole building in forty-three minutes.

"You can imagine the exhausted state Aunt Kate and I are in after travelling five weeks with him. We simply struck in Switzerland and sent him on to Italy alone. I had hoped he would meet us in Valedolmo, but we have been detained here longer than we expected, and now he's rushed off again—where to, goodness only knows; we don't.

"Anyway, Aunt Kate and I shall land in Valedolmo about the end of the week. I am dying to see you; I have some beautiful news that's too complicated to write. We've engaged rooms at the Hotel du Lac—I hope it's decent; it's the only place starred in Baedeker.

"Aunt Kate wishes to be remembered to your father and Miss Hazel.

"Yours ever,

NAN HILLIARD.

"P. S. I'm awfully sorry not to bring Jerry; I know you'd adore him."

She returned the letter to its envelope and looked up. "Now isn't that abominable?" she demanded.

"Abominable!" Miss Hazel was scandalized. "My dear, I think it's delightful."

"Oh, yes—I mean about Jerry Junior; I've been trying for six years to get hold of that man."

Tony behind them made a sudden movement that let out nearly a yard of rope, and the *Farfalla* listed heavily to starboard.

"Tony!" Constance threw over her shoulder. "Don't you know enough to sit still when you are holding the sheet?"

"*Scusi*," he murmured. The sulky look had vanished from his face; he wore an expression of alert attention.

"Of course we shall have them at the villa," said Miss Hazel. "And we shall have to get some new dishes. Elizabetta has already broken so many plates that she has to stop and wash them between courses."

Constance looked dreamily across the lake; she appeared to be thinking. "I wonder," she inquired finally, "if Jerry Junior knew we were here in Valedolmo?"

Her father emerged from the columns of his paper.

"Of course he knew it, and having heard what a dangerous young person you were, he said to himself, 'I'd better keep out.'"

"I wish I knew. It would make the score against him considerably heavier."

"So there is already a score? I hadn't supposed that the game had begun."

She nodded.

"Six years ago—but he doesn't know it. Yes, Dad," her tone was melodramatic, "for six years I've been waiting for Jerry Junior and planning my revenge. And now, when I have him almost in my grasp, he eludes me again!"

"Dear me!" Mr. Wilder ejaculated. "What did the young man do?"

Had Constance turned she would have found Tony's face an interesting study. But she knew well enough without looking at him that he was listening to the conversation, and she determined to give him something to listen to. It was a salutary thing for

Tony to be kept in mind of the fact that there were other men in the world.

She sighed.

"He was the first man I ever loved, Father, and he spurned me. Do you remember that Christmas when I was in boarding-school and you were called South on business? I wanted to visit Nancy Long, but you wouldn't let me because you didn't like her father; and you got Mrs. Jerymn Hilliard whom I had never set eyes on to invite me there? I didn't want to go, and you said I must, and were perfectly horrid about it—you remember that?"

Mr. Wilder grunted.

"Yes, I see you do. And you remember how, with my usual sweetness, I finally gave way? Well, Dad, you never knew the reason. The Yale Glee Club came to Westfield that year just before the holidays began, and Miss Jane let everybody go to the concert whose deportment had been above eighty—that of course included me.

"Well, we all went, and we all fell in love—in a body—with a sophomore who played the banjo and sang negro songs. He had lovely dark gazelle-like eyes and he sang funny songs without smiling. The whole school raved about him all the way home; we cut his picture out of the program and pasted in the front of our watches. His name, Father—" she paused dramatically, "was Jerymn Hilliard Junior!"

"I sat up half the night writing diplomatic letters to you and Mrs. Hilliard; and the next day when it got around that I was actually going to visit in his house—well, I was the most popular girl in school. I was sixteen years old then; I wore sailor suits and my hair was braided down my back. Probably I did look young; and then Nannie, whom I was supposedly visiting, was only fifteen. There were a lot of cousins in the house besides all the little Hilliards, and what do you think? They made the children eat in the schoolroom! I never saw him until Christmas night; then when we were introduced, he shook my hand in a listless sort of way, said 'How d' y' do?' and forgot all about me. He went off with the Glee Club the next day, and I only saw him once more.

"We were playing blind man's buff in the school-room; I had just been caught by the hair. It hurt and I was squealing. Everybody else was clapping and laughing, when suddenly the door burst open and there stood Jerry Junior! He looked straight at me and growled:

"'What are you kids making such an infernal racket about?'"

She shut her eyes.

"Aunt Hazel, Dad, just think. He was my first love. His picture was at that moment in a locket around my neck. And he called me a *kid*!"

"And you've never seen him since?" Miss Hazel's smile expressed amused indulgence.

Constance shook her head.

"He's always been away when I've visited Nan—and for six years I've been waiting." She straightened up with an air of determination. "But now, if he's on the continent of Europe, I'll get him!"

"And what shall you do with him?" her father mildly inquired.

"Do with him? I'll make him take it back; I'll make him eat that word kid!"

"H'm!" said her father. "I hope you'll get him; he might act as an antidote to some of these officers."

They had run in under the shadow of the mountain and the keel grated on the shore. Constance raised her eyes and studied the towering crag above their heads; when she lowered them again, her gaze for an instant met Tony's. There was a new light in his eyes—amusement, triumph, something entirely baffling. He gave her the intangible feeling of having at last got the mastery of the situation.

CHAPTER XI

The sun was setting behind Monte Maggiore, the fishing smacks were coming home, Luigi had long since carried the tea things into the house; but still the two callers lingered on the terrace of Villa Rosa. It was Lieutenant di Ferara's place to go first since he had come first, and Captain Coroloni doggedly held his post until such time as his junior officer should see fit to take himself off. The captain knew, as well as everyone else at the officer's mess, that in the end the lieutenant would be the favored man; for he was a son of Count Guido di Ferara of Turin, and titles are at a premium in the American market. But still the marriage contract was not signed yet, and the fact remained that the captain had come last: accordingly he waited.

They had been there fully two hours, and poor Miss Hazel was worn with the strain. She sat nervously on the edge of her chair, and leaned forward with clasped hands listening intently. It required very keen attention to keep the run of either the captain's or the lieutenant's English. A few days before she had laughed at what seemed to be a funny story, and had later learned that it was an announcement of the death of the lieutenant's grandmother. Today she confined her answers to inarticulate murmurs which might be interpreted as either assents or negations as the case required.

Constance however was buoyantly at her ease; she loved nothing better than the excitement of a difficult situation. As she bridged over pauses, and unobtrusively translated from the officer's English into real English, she at the same time kept a watchful eye on the water. She had her own reasons for wishing to detain the callers until her father's return.

Presently she saw, across the lake, a yellow sailboat float out from the shadow of Monte Maggiore and head in a long tack toward Villa Rosa. With this she gave up the task of keeping the conversation general; and abandoning Captain Coroloni to her aunt, she strolled over to the terrace parapet with Lieutenant di Ferara at her side. The picture they made was a charming color scheme. Constance wore white, the lieutenant pale blue; an oleander tree beside them showed a cloud of pink blossoms, while behind them for a background, appeared the rose of the villa wall and the deep green of cypresses against a sunset sky. The picture was particularly effective as seen from the point of view of an approaching boat.

Constance broke off a spray of oleander, and while she listened to the lieutenant's recountal of a practice march, she picked up his hat from the balustrade and idly arranged the flowers in the vizor. He bent toward her and said something; she responded with a laugh. They were both too occupied to notice that the boat had floated close in shore, until the flap of the falling sail announced its presence. Constance glanced up with a start. She caught her father's eye fixed anxiously upon her; whatever Gustavo and the officer's mess of the tenth cavalry might think, he had not the slightest wish in the world to see his daughter the Contessa di Ferara. Tony's face also wore an expression; he was sober, disgusted, disdainful; there was a glint of anger and determination in his eye. Constance hurried to the water steps to greet her father. Of Tony she took no manner of notice; if a man elects to be a donkey-driver, he must swallow the insults that go with the part.

The officers, observing that Luigi was hovering about the doorway waiting to announce dinner, waived the question of precedence and made their adieus. While Mr. Wilder and Miss Hazel were intent on the captain's labored farewell speech, the lieutenant crossed to Constance who still stood at the head of the water steps. He murmured something in Italian as he bowed over her hand and raised it to his lips. Constance blushed very becomingly as she drew her hand away; she was aware, if the officer was not, that Tony was standing beside them looking on. But as he raised his eyes, he too became aware of it; the man's expression was more than impertinent. The lieutenant stepped to his side and said something low and rapid, something which should have made a right-minded donkey-driver touch his hat and slink off. But Tony held his ground with a laugh which was more impertinent than the stare had been. The lieutenant's face flushed angrily and his hand half instinctively went to his sword. Constance stepped forward.

"Tony! I shall have no further need of your services. You may go."

Tony suddenly came to his senses.

"I—beg your pardon, Miss Wilder," he stammered.

"I shall not want you again; please go." She turned her back and joined the others.

The two officers with final salutes took themselves off. Miss Hazel hurried indoors to make ready for dinner; Mr. Wilder followed in her wake, muttering something about finding the change to pay Tony. Constance stood where they left her, staring at the pavement with hotly burning cheeks.

"Miss Wilder!" Tony crossed to her side; his manner was humble—actually humble—the usual mocking undertone in his voice was missing. "Really I'm awfully sorry to have caused you annoyance; it was unpardonable."

Constance turned toward him.

"Yes, Tony, I think it was. Your position does not give you the right to insult my guests."

Tony stiffened slightly.

"I acknowledge that I insulted him, and I'm sorry. But he insulted me, for the matter of that. I didn't like the way he looked at me, any more than he liked the way I looked at him."

"There is a certain deference, Tony, which an officer in the Royal Italian Army has a right to expect from a donkey-driver."

Tony shrugged.

"It is a difficult position to hold, Miss Wilder. A donkey-driver, I find, plays the same accommodating rôle as the family watch-dog. You pat him when you choose; you kick him when you choose; and he is supposed to swallow both attentions with equal grace."

"You should have chosen another profession."

"Naturally, I was not flattered to find that your real reason for staying at home today, was that you were expecting more entertaining callers."

"Is there any use in discussing it further? I am not going to climb any more mountains, and I shall not, as I told you, need a donkey-man again."

"Then I'm discharged?"

"If you wish to put it so. You must see for yourself that the play has gone far enough. However, it has been amusing, and we will at least part friends."

She held out her hand; it was a mark of definite dismissal rather than a token of friendly forgiveness.

Tony bowed over her hand in perfect mimicry of the lieutenant's manner. "Signorina, *addio*!" He gravely raised it to his lips.

She snatched her hand away quickly and without glancing at him turned toward the house. He let her cross half the terrace then he called softly:

"Signorina!"

She kept on without pausing. He took a quick step after.

"Signorina, a moment!"

She half turned.

"Well?"

"I beg of you—one little favor. There are two American ladies expected at the Hotel du Lac and I thought—perhaps—would you mind writing me a letter of recommendation?"

Constance turned back without a word and walked into the house.

Mr. Wilder's conversation at dinner that night was of the day's excursion and Tony. He was elated, enthusiastic, glowing.

Mountain-climbing was the most interesting pursuit in the world; he would begin tomorrow and exhaust the Alps. And as for Tony—his intelligence, his discretion, his cleverness—there never had been such a guide. Constance listened silently, her eyes on her plate. At another time it might have occurred to her that her father's enthusiasm was excessive, but tonight she was occupied with her thoughts, and she had no reason in the world to suspect him of guile. She decided, however, to postpone the announcement of Tony's dismissal; tomorrow mountain-climbing might look less alluring.

Dinner over, Mr. Wilder with a tired if satisfied sigh, dropped into a chair to finish his reading of the London *Times*. He no longer skimmed his paper lightly as in the days when papers were to be had hot at any hour. He read it carefully, painstakingly, from the first advertisement to the last obituary; and he laid it down in the end with a disappointed sigh that there were not more residential properties for hire, that the day's death list was so meager.

Miss Hazel settled herself to her knitting. She was making a rain-bow shawl of seven colors and an intricate pattern, and she had to count her stitches; conversation was impossible. Constance, vaguely restless, picked up a book and laid it down, and finally sauntered out to the terrace with no thought in the world but to see the moon rise over the mountains.

As she approached the parapet she became aware that someone was lounging on the water-steps smoking a cigarette. The smoker rose politely but ventured no remark.

"Is that you, Giuseppe?" she asked in Italian.

"No, signorina. It is I—Tony. I am waiting for orders."

"For orders!" There was astonishment as well as indignation in her tone. "I thought I made it clear—"

"That I was discharged? Yes, signorina. But I have been so fortunate as to find another place. The Signor Papa has engage me. I go wif him; we climb all ze mountain around." He waved his hand largely to comprise the whole landscape. "I sink perhaps it is better so—for the Signor Papa and me to go alone. Mountain climbing is too hard; zere is too much fatigue, signorina, for you."

He bowed humbly and deferentially, and retired to the steps and his cigarette.

CHAPTER XII

Half past six on the following morning found Constance and her father rising from the breakfast table and Tony turning in at the gate. Constance's nod of greeting was barely perceptible, and her father's eye contained a twinkle as he watched her. Tony studied her mountain-climbing costume with an air of concern.

"You go wif us, signorina?" His expression was blended of surprise and disapproval, but in spite of himself his tone was triumphant. "You say to me yesterday you no want to climb any more mountain."

"I have changed my mind."

"But zis mountain today too long, too high. You get tired, signorina. Perhaps anozzer day we take li'l' baby mountain, zen you can go."

"I am going today."

"It is not possible, signorina. I have not brought ze donk'."

"Oh, I'm going to walk."

"As you please, signorina."

He sighed patiently. Then he looked up and caught her eye. They both laughed.

"Signorina," he whispered, "I ver' happy today. Zat Costantina she more kind. Yesterday ver' unkind; I go home ver' sad. But today I sink—"

"Yes?"

"I sink after all maybe she like me li'l' bit."

* * *

Giuseppe rowed the three climbers a mile or so down the lake and set them ashore at the base of their mountain. They started up gaily and had accomplished half their journey before they thought of being tired. Tony surpassed himself; if he had been entertaining the day before he was doubly so now. His spirits were bubbling over and contagious. He and Constance acted like two children out of school. They ran races and talked to the peasants in the wayside cottages. They drove a herd of goats for half a mile while the goatherd strolled behind and smoked Tony's cigarettes. Constance took a water jar from a little girl they met coming from the fountain and endeavored to balance it on her own head, with the result that she nearly drowned both herself and the child.

They finally stopped for luncheon in a grove of chestnut trees with sheep nibbling on the hillside below them and a shepherd boy somewhere out of sight playing on a mouth organ. It should have been a flute, but they were in a forgiving mood. Constance this time did her share of the work. She and Tony together spread the cloth and made the coffee while her father fanned himself and looked on. If Mr. Wilder had any unusual thoughts in regard to the donkey-man, they were at least not reflected in his face.

When they had finished their meal Tony spread his coat under a tree.

"Signorina," he said, "perhaps you li'l' tired? Look, I make nice place to sleep. You lie down and rest while ze Signor Papa and me, we have li'l' smoke. Zen after one, two hours I come call you."

Constance very willingly accepted the suggestion. They had walked five uphill miles since morning. It was two hours later that she opened her eyes to find Tony bending over her. She sat up and regarded him sternly. He had the grace to blush.

"Tony, did you kiss my hand?"

"*Scusi*, signorina. I ver' sorry to wake you, but it is tree o'clock and ze Signor Papa he say we must start just now or we nevair get to ze top."

"Answer my question."

"Signorina, I cannot tell to you a lie. It is true, I forget I am just poor donkey-man. I play li'l' game. You sleeping beauty; I am ze prince. I come to wake you. Just *one* kiss I drop on your hand—one ver' little kiss, signorina."

Constance assumed an air of indignant reproof but in the midst of it she laughed.

"I wish you wouldn't be so funny, Tony; I can't scold you as much as you deserve. But I am angry just the same, and if anything like that ever happens again I shall be very *very* angry.

"Signorina, I would not make you very *very* angry for anysing. As long as I live nosing like zat shall happen again. No, nevair, I promise."

They plunged into a pine wood and climbed for another two hours, the summit always vanishing before them like a mirage. At the end of that time they were apparently no nearer their goal than when they had started. They had followed first one path, then another, until they had lost all sense of direction, and finally when they came to a place where three paths diverged, they had to acknowledge themselves definitely lost. Mr. Wilder elected one path, Tony another, and Constance sat down on a rock.

"I'm not going any farther," she observed.

"You can't stay here all night," said her father.

"Well, I can't walk over this mountain all night. We don't get anywhere; we merely move in circles. I don't think much of the guide you engaged. He doesn't know his way."

"He wasn't engaged to know his way," Tony retorted. "He was engaged to wear earrings and sing Santa Lucia."

Constance continued to sit on her rock while Tony went forward on a reconnoitering expedition. He returned in ten minutes with the information that there was a shepherd's hut not very far off with a shepherd inside who would like to be friendly. If the signorina would deign to ask some questions in the Italian language which she spoke so fluently, they could doubtless obtain directions as to the way home.

They found the shepherd, the shepherdess and four little shepherds eating their evening polenta in an earth-floored room, with half a dozen chickens and the family pig gathered about them in an expectant group. They rose politely and invited the travellers to enter. It was an event in their simple lives when foreigners presented themselves at the door.

Constance commenced amenities by announcing that she had been walking on the mountain since sunrise and was starving. Did they by chance have any fresh milk?

"Starving! *Madonna mia*, how dreadful!" Madame held up her hands. But yes, to be sure they had fresh milk. They kept four cows. That was their business—turning milk into cheese and selling it on market day in the village. Also they had some fresh mountain strawberries which Beppo had gathered that morning—perhaps they too might be pleasing to the signorina?

Constance nodded affirmatively, and added, with her eyes on the pig, that it might be pleasanter to eat outside where they could look at the view. She became quite gay again over what she termed their afternoon tea-party, and her father had to remind her most insistently that if they wished to get down before darkness overtook them they must start at once. An Italian twilight is short. They paid for the food and presented a lira apiece to the children, leaving them silhouetted against the sky in a bobbing row shouting musical farewells.

Their host led them through the woods and out on to the brow of the mountain in order to start them down by the right path. He regretted that he could not go all the way but the sheep had still to be brought in for the night. At the parting he was garrulous with directions.

The easiest way to get home now would be straight down the mountain to Grotta del Monte—he pointed out the brown-tiled roofs of a village far below them—there they could find donkeys or an ox-cart to take them back. It was nine kilometres to Valedolmo. They had come quite out of their way; if they had taken the right path in the morning they would have reached the top where the view was magnificant—truly magnificant. It was a pity to miss it. Perhaps some other day they would like to come again and he himself would be pleased to guide them. He shook hands and wished them a pleasant journey. They would best hurry a trifle, he added, for darkness came fast and when one got caught on the mountain at night—he shrugged his shoulders and looked at Tony—one needed a guide who knew his business.

They had walked for ten minutes when they heard someone shouting behind and found a young man calling to them to wait. He caught up with them and breathlessly explained.

Pasquale had told him that they were foreigners from America who were climbing the mountain for diversion and who had lost their way. He was going down to the village himself and would be pleased to guide them.

He fell into step beside Constance and commenced asking questions, while Tony, as the path was narrow, perforce fell behind. Occasionally Constance translated, but usually she laughed without translating, and Tony, for the twentieth time, found himself hating the Italian language.

The young man's questions were refreshingly ingenuous. He was curious about America, since he was thinking, he said, of becoming an American himself some day. He knew a man once who had gone to America to live and had made a fortune there—but yes a large fortune—ten thousand lire in four years. Perhaps the signorina knew him—Giuseppe Motta; he lived in Buenos Aires. And what did it look like—America? How was it different from Italy?

Constance described the skyscrapers in New York.

His wonder was intense. A building twenty stories high! *Dio mio*! He should hate to mount himself up all those stairs. Were the buildings like that in the country too? Did the shepherds live in houses twenty stories high?

"Oh no," she laughed. "In the country the houses are just like these only they are made of wood instead of stone."

"Of wood?" He opened his eyes. "But signorina, do they never burn?"

He had another question to ask. He had been told—though

of course he did not believe it—that the Indians in America had red skins.

Constance nodded yes. His eyes opened wider.

"Truly red like your coat?" with a glance at her scarlet golf jacket.

"Not quite," she admitted.

"But how it must be diverting," he sighed, "to travel the world over and see different things." He fell silent and trudged on beside her, the wanderlust in his eyes.

It was almost dark when they reached the big arched gateway that led into the village. Here their ways parted and they paused for farewell.

"Signorina," the young man said suddenly, "take me with you back to America. I will prune your olive trees, I will tend your vines. You can leave me in charge when you go on your travels."

She shook her head with a laugh.

"But I have no vines; I have no olive trees. You would be homesick for Italy."

He shrugged his shoulders.

"Then good bye. You, signorina, will go around the world and see many sights while I, for travel, shall ride on a donkey to Valedolmo."

He shook hands all around and with the grace of a prince accepted two of Tony's cigarettes. His parting speech showed him a fatalist.

"What will be, will be. There is a girl—" he waved his hand vaguely in the direction of the village. "If I go to America then I cannot stay behind and marry Maria. So perhaps it is planned for the best. You will find me, signorina, when next you come to Italy, still digging the ground in Grotta del Monte."

As he swung away Tony glanced after him with a suggestion of malice, then he transferred his gaze to the empty gateway.

"I see no one else with whom you can talk Italian. Perhaps for ten minutes you will deign to speak English with me?"

"I am too tired to talk," she threw over her shoulder as she followed her father through the gate.

They plunged into a tangle of tortuous paved streets, the houses pressing each other as closely as if there were not all the outside world to spread in. Grotta del Monte is built on a slope and its streets are in reality long narrow flights of stairs all converging in the little piazza. The moon was not yet up, and aside from an occasional flickering light before a madonna's shrine, the way was black.

"Signorina, take my arm. I'm afraid maybe you fall."

Tony's voice was humbly persuasive. Constance laughed and laid her hand lightly on his arm. Tony dropped his own hand over hers and held her firmly. Neither spoke until they came to the piazza.

"Signorina," he whispered, "you make me ver' happy tonight."

She drew her hand away.

"I'm tired, Tony. I'm not quite myself."

"No, signorina, yesterday I sink maybe you not yourself, but to-day you ver' good ver' kind—jus' your own self ze way you ought to be."

The piazza, after the dark, narrow streets that led to it, seemed bubbling with life. The day's work was finished and the evening's play had begun. In the center, where a fountain splashed into a broad bowl, groups of women and girls with copper water-jars were laughing and gossiping as they waited their turns. One side of the square was flanked by the imposing façade of a church with the village saint on a pedestal in front; the other side, by a cheerfully inviting osteria with tables and chairs set into the street and a glimpse inside of a blazing hearth and copper kettles.

Mr. Wilder headed in a straight line for the nearest chair and dropped into it with an expression of permanence. Constance followed and they held a colloquy with a bowing host. He was vague as to the finding of carriage or donkeys, but if they would accommodate themselves until after supper there would be a diligence along which would take them back to Valedolmo.

"How soon will the diligence arrive?" asked Constance.

The man spread out his hands.

"It is due in three quarters of an hour, but it may be early and it may be late. It arrives when God and the driver wills."

"In that case," she laughed, "we will accommodate ourselves until after supper—and we have appetites! Please bring everything you have."

They supped on *minestra* and *fritto misto* washed down with the red wine of Grotta del Monte, which, their host assured them, was famous through all the country. He could not believe that they had never heard of it in Valedolmo. People sent for it from far off; even from Verona.

They finished their supper and the famous wine, but there was still no diligence. The village also had finished its supper and was drifting in family groups into the piazza. The moon was just showing above the house-tops, and its light, combined with the blazing braziers before the cook-shops made the square a patch work of brilliant high-lights and black shadows from deep cut doorways. Constance sat up alertly and watched the people crowding past. Across from the inn an itinerant show had established itself on a rudely improvised stage, with two flaring torches which threw their light half across the piazza, and turned the spray of the fountain into an iridescent shower. The gaiety of the scene was contagious. Constance rose insistently.

"Come, Dad; let's go over and see what they're doing."

"No, thank you, my dear. I prefer my chair."

"Oh, Dad, you're so phlegmatic!"

"But I thought you were tired."

"I'm not any more; I want to see the play.—You come then, Tony."

Tony rose with an elaborate sigh.

"As you please, signorina," he murmured obediently. An onlooker would have thought Constance cruel in dragging him away from his well-earned rest.

They made their way across the piazza and mounted the church steps behind the crowd where they could look across obliquely to the little stage. A clown was dancing to the music of a hurdy-gurdy while a woman in a tawdry pink satin evening gown beat an accompaniment on a drum. It was a very poor play with very poor players, and yet it represented to these people of Grotta del Monte something of life, of the big outside world which they in their little village would never see. Their upturned faces touched by the moonlight and the flare of the torches contained a look of wondering eagerness—the same look that had been in the eyes of the young peasant when he had begged to be taken to America.

The two stood back in the shadow of the doorway watching the people with the same interest that the people were expending on the stage. A child had been lifted to the base of the saint's pedestal in order to see, and in the excitement of a duel between two clowns he suddenly lost his balance and toppled off. His mother snatched him up quickly and commenced covering the hurt arm with kisses to make it well.

Constance laughed.

"Isn't it queer," she asked, "to think how different these people are from us and yet how exactly the same. Their way of living is absolutely foreign but their feelings are just like yours and mine."

He touched her arm and called her attention to a man and a girl on the step below them. It was the young peasant again who had guided them down the mountain, but who now had eyes for no one but Maria. She leaned toward him to see the stage and his arm was around her. Their interest in the play was purely a pretense and both of them knew it.

Tony laughed softly and echoed her words.

"Yes, their feelings are just like yours and mine."

He slipped his arm around her.

Constance drew back quickly.

"I think," she remarked, "that the diligence has come."

"Oh, hang the diligence!" Tony growled. "Why couldn't it have been five minutes late?"

They returned to the inn to find Mr. Wilder already on the front seat, and obligingly holding the reins, while the driver occupied himself with a glass of the famous wine. The diligence was a roomy affair of four seats and three horses. Behind the driver were three Italians gesticulating violently over local politics; a new *sindaco* was imminent. Behind these were three black-hooded nuns covertly interested in the woman in the pink evening gown. And behind the three, occupying the exact center of the rear seat, was a fourth nun with the portly bearing of a Mother Superior. She was very comfortable as she was, and did not propose to move. Constance climbed up on one side of her and Tony on the other.

"We are well chaperoned," he grumbled, as they jolted out of the piazza. "I always did think that the Church interfered too much with the rights of individuals."

Constance, in a spirit of friendly expansiveness, proceeded to pick up an acquaintance with the nuns, and the four black heads were presently bobbing in unison, while Tony, in gloomy isolation at his end of the seat, folded his arms and stared at the road. The driver had passed through many villages that day and had drunk many glasses of famous wine; he cracked his whip and sang as he drove. They rattled in and out of stone-paved villages, along open stretches of moonlit road, past villas and olive groves. Children screamed after them, dogs barked, Constance and her four nuns were very vivacious, and Tony's gloom deepened with every mile.

They had covered three quarters of the distance when the diligence was brought to a halt before a high stone wall and a solid barred gate. The nuns came back to the present with an excited cackling. Who would believe they had reached the convent so soon! They made their adieus and ponderously descended, their departure accelerated by Tony who had become of a sudden alertly helpful. As they started again he slid along into the Mother Superior's empty seat.

"What were we saying when the diligence interrupted?" he inquired.

"I don't remember, Tony, but I don't want to talk any

more; I'm tired."

"You tired, signorina? Lay your head on my shoulder and go to sleep."

"Tony, *please* behave yourself. I'm simply too tired to make you do it."

He reached over and took her hand. She did not try to withdraw it for two—three minutes; then she shot him a sidewise glance.

"Tony," she said, "don't you think you are forgetting your place?"

"No, signorina, I am just learning it."

"Let go my hand."

He gazed pensively at the moon and hummed Santa Lucia under his breath.

"Tony! I shall be angry with you."

"I shall be ver' sorry for zat, signorina. I do not wish to make you angry, but I sink—perhaps you get over it."

"You are behaving abominably today, Tony. I shall never stay alone with you again."

"Signorina, look at zat moon up dere. Is it not ver' bright? When I look at zat moon I have always beautiful toughts about how much I love Costantina."

An interval followed during which neither spoke. The driver's song was growing louder and the horses were galloping. The diligence suddenly rounded a curved cliff on two wheels. Constance lurched against him; he caught her and held her. Her lips were very near his; he kissed her softly.

She moved to the far end of the seat and faced him with flushed cheeks.

"I thought you were a gentleman!"

"I used to be, signorina; now I am only poor donkey-man."

"I shall never speak to you again. You can climb as many mountains as you wish with my father, but you can't have anything more to do with me."

"*Scusi*, signorina. I—I did not mean to. It was just an accident, signorina."

Constance turned her back and stared at the road.

"It was not my fault. Truly it was not my fault. I did not wish to kiss you—no nevair. But I could not help it. You put your head too close."

She raised her eyes and studied the mountain-top.

"Signorina, why you treat me so cruel?"

Her back was inflexible.

"I am desolate. If you forgive me zis once I will nevair again do a sing so wicked. Nevair, nevair, nevair."

Constance continued her inspection of the mountain-top. Tony leaned forward until he could see her face.

"Signorina," he whispered, "jus' give me one li'l' smile to show me you are not angry forever."

The stage had stopped and Mr. Wilder was climbing down but Constance's gaze was still fixed on the sky, and Tony's eyes were on her.

"What's the matter, Constance, have you gone to sleep? Aren't you going to get out?"

She came back with a start.

"Are we here already?"

There was a suspicion of regret in her tone which did not escape Tony.

At the Villa Rosa gates he wished them a humbly deferential good-night but with a smile hovering about the corners of his mouth. Constance made no response. As he strode off, however, she turned her head and looked after him. He turned too and caught her. He waved his hand with a laugh, and took up his way, whistling Santa Lucia in double time.

CHAPTER XIII

Three days passed in which Mr. Wilder and Tony industriously climbed, and in which nothing of consequence passed between Constance and Tony. If she happened to be about when the expeditions either started or came to an end (and for one reason or another she usually was) she ignored him entirely; and he ignored her, except for an occasional mockingly deferential bow. He appeared to extract as much pleasure from the excursions as Mr. Wilder, and he asked for no extra compensation by the way.

It was Tuesday again, just a week and a day since the young American had dropped over the wall of Villa Rosa asking for the garden of the prince. Tony and Mr. Wilder were off on a trip; Miss Hazel and Constance on the point of sitting down to afternoon tea—there were no guests today—when the gardener from the Hotel du Lac appeared with a message from Nannie Hilliard. She and her aunt had arrived half an hour before, which was a good two days earlier than they were due. Constance read the note with a clouded brow and silently passed it to Miss Hazel. The news was not so entirely welcome as under other circumstances it would have been. Nannie Hilliard was both perspicacious and fascinating, and Constance foresaw that her presence would tangle further the already tangled plot of the little comedy which was unfolding itself at Villa Rosa. But Miss Hazel, divining nothing of comedies or plots, was thrown into a pleasant flutter by the news. Guests were a luxury which occurred but seldom in the quiet monotony of Valedolmo.

"We must call on them at once and bring them back to the house."

"I suppose we must." Constance agreed with an uncordial sigh.

Fifteen minutes later they were on their way to the Hotel du

Lac, while Elizabetta, on her knees in the villa guest-room, was vigorously scrubbing the mosaic floor.

Gustavo hurried out to meet them. He was plainly in a flutter; something had occurred to upset the usual suavity of his manners.

"*Si*, signorina, in ze garden—ze two American ladies—having tea. And you are acquaint wif ze family; all ze time you are acquaint wif zem, and you never tell me!" There was mystification and reproach in his tone.

Constance eyed him with a degree of mystification on her side.

"I am acquainted with a number of families that I have never told you about," she observed.

"*Scusi*, signorina," he stammered; and immediately, "Tony, zat donk'-man, what you do wif him?"

"Oh, he and my father are climbing Monte Brione today."

"What time zay come home?"

"About seven o'clock, I fancy."

"Ze signora and ze signorina—zay come two days before zay are expect." He was clearly aggrieved by the fact.

Constance's mystification increased; she saw not the slightest connection.

"I suppose, Gustavo, you can find them something to eat even if they did come two days before they were expected?"

The two turned toward the arbor, but Constance paused for a moment and glanced back with a shade of mischief in her eye.

"By the way, Gustavo, that young man who taught the parrot English has gone?"

Gustavo rolled his eyes to the sky and back to her face. She understood nothing; was there ever a muddle like this?

"*Si*, signorina," he murmured confusedly, "ze yong man is gone."

Nannie caught sight of the visitors first, and with a start which nearly upset the tea table, came running forward to meet them; while her aunt, Mrs. Eustace, followed more placidly. Nannie was a big wholesome outdoor girl of a purely American type.

She waited for no greetings; she had news to impart.

"Nannie caught sight of the visitors first, and came running forward to meet them"

"Constance, Miss Hazel! I'm so glad to see you—what do you think? I'm engaged!"

Miss Hazel murmured incoherent congratulations, and tried not to look as shocked as she felt. In her day, no lady would have made so delicate an announcement in any such off-hand manner as this. Constance received it in the spirit in which it was given.

"Who's the man?" she inquired, as she shook hands with Mrs. Eustace.

"You don't know him—Harry Eastman, a friend of Jerry's. Jerry doesn't know it yet, and I had to confide in someone. Oh, it's no secret; Harry cabled home—he wanted to get it announced so I couldn't change my mind. You see he only had a three weeks' vacation; he took a fast boat, landed at Cherbourg, followed us the whole length of France, and caught us in Lucerne just after Jerry had gone. I couldn't refuse him after he'd taken such a lot of trouble. That's what detained us: we had expected to come a week ago. And now—" by a rapid change of expression she became tragic—"We've lost Jerry Junior!"

"Lost Jerry Junior!" Constance's tone was interested. "What has become of him?"

"We haven't an idea. He's been spirited off—vanished from the earth and left no trace. Really, we're beginning to be afraid he's been captured by brigands. That head waiter, that Gustavo, knows where he is, but we can't get a word out of him. He tells a different story every ten minutes. I looked in the register to see if by chance he'd left an address there, and what do you think I found?"

"Oh!" said Constance; there was a world of illumination in her tone. "What did you find?" she asked, hastily suppressing every emotion but polite curiosity.

"'Abraham Lincoln' in Jerry's hand-writing!"

"Really!" Constance dimpled irrepressibly. "You are sure Jerry wrote it?"

"It was his writing; and I showed it to Gustavo, and what do you think he said?"

Constance shook her head.

"He said that Jerry had forgotten to register, that that was written by a Hungarian nobleman who was here last week—imagine a Hungarian nobleman named Abraham Lincoln!"

Constance dropped into one of the little iron chairs and bowed her head on the back and laughed.

"Perhaps you can explain?" There was a touch of sharpness in Nannie's tone.

"Don't ever ask me to explain anything Gustavo says; the man is not to be believed under oath."

"But what's become of Jerry?"

"Oh, he'll turn up." Constance's tone was comforting. "Aunt Hazel," she called. Miss Hazel and Mrs. Eustace, their heads together over the tea table, were busily making up three months' dropped news. "Do you remember the young man I told you about who popped into our garden last week? That was

Jerry Junior!"

"Then you've seen him?" said Nannie.

Constance related the episode of the broken wall—the sequel she omitted. "I hadn't seen him for six years," she added apologetically, "and I didn't recognize him. Of course if I'd dreamed—"

Nannie groaned.

"And I thought I'd planned it so beautifully!"

"Planned what?"

"I suppose I might as well tell you since it's come to nothing. We hoped—that is, you see—I've been so worried for fear Jerry—" She took a breath and began again. "You know, Constance, when it comes to getting married, a man has no more sense than a two-year child. So I determined to pick out a wife for Jerry, myself, one I would like to have for a sister. I've done it three times and he simply wouldn't look at them; you can't imagine how stubborn he is. But when I found we were coming to Valedolmo, I said to myself, now this is my opportunity; I will have him marry Connie Wilder."

"You might have asked my permission."

"Oh, well, Jerry's a dear; next to Harry you couldn't find anyone nicer. But I knew the only way was not to let him suspect. I thought you see that you were still staying at the hotel; I didn't know you'd taken a villa, so I planned for him to come to meet us three days before we really expected to get here. I thought in the meantime, being stranded together in a little hotel you'd surely get acquainted—Jerry's very resourceful that way—and with all this beautiful Italian scenery about, and nothing to do—"

"I see!" Constance's tone was somewhat dry.

"But nothing happened as I had planned. You weren't here, he was bored to death, and I was detained longer than I meant. We got the most pathetic letter from him the second day, saying there was no one but the head waiter to talk to, nothing but an india-rubber tree to look at, and if we didn't come immediately, he'd do the Dolomites without us. Then finally, just as we were on the point of leaving, he sent a telegram saying: 'Don't come. Am climbing mountains. Stay there till you hear from me.' But being already packed, we came, and this is what we find—" She waved her hand over the empty grove.

"It serves you right; you shouldn't deceive people."

"It was for Jerry's good—and yours too. But what shall we do? He doesn't know we're here and he has left no address."

"Come out to the villa and visit us till he comes to search for you."

Constance could hear her aunt delivering the same invitation to Mrs. Eustace, and she perforce repeated it, though with the inward hope that it would be declined. She had no wish that Tony and her father should return from their trip to find a family party assembled on the terrace. The adventure was not to end with any such tame climax as that. To her relief they did decline, at least for the night; they could make no definite plans until they had heard from Jerry. Constance rose upon this assurance and precipitated their leave-takings; she did not wish her aunt to press them to change their minds.

"Good-bye, Mrs. Eustace, good-bye, Nannie; we'll be around tonight to take you sailing—provided there's any breeze."

She nodded and dragged her aunt off; but as they were entering the arbor a plan for further complicating matters popped into her head, and she turned back to call:

"You are coming to the villa tomorrow, remember, whether Jerry Junior turns up or not. I'll write a note and invite him too—Gustavo can give it to him when he comes, and you needn't bother any more about him."

They found Gustavo hovering omnivorously in the courtyard, hungering for news; Constance summoned him to her side.

"Gustavo, I am going to send you a note tonight for Mr. Jerymn Hilliard. You will see that it gets to him as soon as he arrives?"

"Meestair Jayreem Ailyar?" Gustavo stared.

"Yes, the brother of the signorina who came today. He is expected tomorrow or perhaps the day after."

"*Scusi*, signorina. You—you acquaint wif him?"

"Yes, certainly. I have known him for six years. Don't forget to deliver the note; it's important."

They raised their parasols and departed, while Gustavo stood in the gateway bowing. The motion was purely mechanical; his thoughts were laboring elsewhere.

CHAPTER XIV

Constance occupied herself upon their return to Villa Rosa in writing the letter to Jerry Junior. It had occurred to her that this was an excellent chance to punish him, and it was the working philosophy of her life that a man should always be punished when opportunity presented. Tony had been entirely too unconcerned during the past few days; he needed a lesson. She spent three quarters of an hour in composing her letter and tore up two false starts before she was satisfied. It did not contain the slightest hint that she knew the truth, and—considered in this light—it was likely to have a chastening effect. The letter ran:

"Villa Rosa, Valedolmo,
"Lago di Garda.

"Dear Jerry Junior: I hope you don't mind being called "Jerry Junior," but "Mr. Hilliard" sounds so absurdly formal, when I have known your sister so long and so well. We are spending the summer here in Valedolmo, and Mrs. Eustace and Nannie have promised to stop with us for a few days, provided you can be persuaded to pause in your mad rush through Europe. Now please take pity on us—guests are such unusual luxuries, and as for *men*! Besides a passing tourist or so, we have had nothing but Italian officers. You can climb mountains with my father—Nan says you are a climber—and we can supply mountains enough to keep you occupied for a month.

"My father would write himself, only that he is climbing this moment.

"Yours most cordially,

"CONSTANCE WILDER."

"P. S. I forgot to mention that we are acquainted already, you and I. We met six years ago, and you insulted me—under your own roof. You called me a *kid*. I shall accept nothing but a personal apology."

Having read it critically, she sealed and addressed it with malicious delight; it was calculated to arouse just about the emotions she would like to have Tony entertain. She gave the note to Giuseppe with instructions to place it in Gustavo's hands, and then settled herself gaily to await results.

Giuseppe was barely out of sight when the two Alpine-climbers appeared at the gate. Constance had been wondering how she could inform Tony that his aunt and sister had arrived, without unbending from the dignified silence of the past three days. The obvious method was to announce it to her father in Tony's presence, but her father slipped into the house by the back way without affording her an opportunity. It was Tony himself who solved the difficulty. Of his own accord he crossed the terrace and approached her side. He laid a bunch of edelweiss on the balustrade.

"It's a peace offering," he observed.

She looked at him a moment without speaking. There was a new expression in her eyes that puzzled Tony, just as the expression in his eyes that morning on the water had puzzled her. She was studying him in the light of Jerry Junior. The likeness to the sophomore, who six years before sang the funny songs without a smile, was so very striking, she wondered she could ever have overlooked it.

"Thank you, Tony; it is very nice of you." She picked up the flowers and smiled—with the knowledge of the letter that was waiting for him she could afford to be forgiving.

"You discharged me, signorina; will you take me back into your service?"

"I am not going to climb any more mountains; it is too fatiguing. I think it is better for you and my father to go alone."

"I will serve you in other ways."

Constance studied the mountains a moment. Should she tell him she knew, or should she keep up the pretense a little longer? Her insatiable love of intrigue won.

"Are you sure you wish to be taken back?"

"*Si*, signorina, I am very sure."

"Then perhaps you will do me a favor on your way home tonight?"

"You have but to ask."

"I wish to send a message to a young American man who is staying at the Hotel du Lac—you may have seen him?"

Tony nodded.

"I have climb Monte Maggiore wif him. You recommend me; I sank you ver' moch. Nice man, zat yong American; ver' good, ver' simpatico." He leaned forward with a sudden air of anxiety. "Signorina, you—you like zat yong man?"

"I have only met him twice, but—yes, I like him."

"You like him better zan me?" His anxiety deepened; he hung upon her words.

She shook her head reassuringly.

"I like you both exactly the same."

"Signorina, which you like better, zat yong American or ze Signor Lieutenant?"

"Your questions are getting too personal, Tony."

He folded his arms and sighed.

"Will you deliver my message?"

"*Si*, signorina, wif pleasure." There was not a trace of curiosity in his expression, nothing beyond a deferential desire to serve.

"Tell him, Tony, that Miss Wilder will be at home tomorrow afternoon at tea time; if he will come by the gate and present a card she will be most pleased to see him. She wishes him to meet an American friend, a Miss Hilliard, who has just arrived at the hotel this afternoon."

She watched him sharply; his expression did not alter by a shade. He repeated the message and then added as if by the merest chance:

"Ze yong American man, signorina—you know his name?"

"Yes, I know his name." This time for the fraction of a second she surprised a look. "His name—" she hesitated tantalizingly—"is Signor Abraham Lincoln."

"Signor Ab-ra-ham Lin-coln." He repeated it after her as if committing it to memory. They gazed at each other soberly a moment; then both laughed and looked away.

Luigi had appeared in the doorway. Seeing no one more important than Tony about, he found no reason for delaying the announcement of dinner.

"*Il pranzo è sulla tavola, signorina.*"

"*Bene*!" said Constance over her shoulder. She turned back to Tony; her manner was kind. "If you go to the kitchen, Tony, Elizabetta will give you some dinner."

"Sank you, signorina." His manner was humble. "Elizabetta's dinners consist of a plate of garlic and macaroni on the kitchen steps. I don't like garlic and I'm tired of macaroni; if it's just the same to you, I think I'll dine at home." He held out his hand.

She read his purpose in his eye and put her own hands behind her.

"You won't shake hands, signorina? We are not friends?"

"I learned a lesson the last time."

"You shake hands wif Lieutenant Count Carlo di Ferara."

"It is the custom in Italy."

"We are in Italy."

"Behave yourself, Tony, and run along home!"

She laughed and nodded and turned away. On the steps she paused to add:

"Be sure not to forget the message for Signor Abraham Lincoln. I shall be disappointed if he doesn't come."

CHAPTER XV

Tony returned to the Hotel du Lac, modestly, by the back way. He assured himself that his aunt and sister were well by means of an open window in the rear of the dining-room. The window was shaded by a clump of camellias, and he studied at his ease the back of Mrs. Eustace's head and Nannie's vivacious profile as she talked in fluent and execrable German to the two Alpinists who were, at the moment, the only other guests. Brotherly affection—and a humorous desire to create a sensation—prompted him to walk in and surprise them. But saner second thoughts prevailed; he decided to postpone the reunion until he should have changed from the picturesque costume of Tony, to the soberer garb of Jerry Junior.

He skirted the dining-room by a wide detour, and entered the court-yard at the side. Gustavo, who for the last hour and a half had been alertly watchful of four entrances at once, pounced upon him and drew him to a corner.

"Signore," in a conspiratorial whisper, "zay are come, ze aunt and ze sister."

"I know—the Signorina Costantina told me so."

Gustavo blinked.

"But, signore, she does not know it."

"Yes, she does—she saw 'em herself."

"I mean, signore, she does not know zat you are ze brover?"

"Oh, no, she doesn't know that."

"But she tell me zat she is acquaint wif ze brover for six years." He shook his head hopelessly.

"That's all right." Tony patted his shoulder reassuringly. "When she knew me I used to have yellow hair, but I thought it made me look too girlish, so I had it dyed black. She didn't recognize me."

Gustavo accepted the explanation with a side glance at the hair.

"Now, pay attention." Tony's tone was slow and distinct.

"I am going upstairs to change my clothes. Then I will slip out the back way with a suit case, and go down the road and meet the omnibus as it comes back from the boat landing. You keep my aunt and sister in the court-yard talking to the parrot or something until the omnibus arrives. Then when I get out, you come forward with your politest bow and ask me if I want a room. I'll attend to the rest—do you understand?"

Gustavo nodded with glistening eyes. He had always felt stirring within him powers for diplomacy, for finesse, and he rose to the occasion magnificently.

Tony turned away and went bounding upstairs two steps at a time, chuckling as he went. He, too, was developing an undreamed of appetite for intrigue, and his capacity in that direction was expanding to meet it. He had covered the first flight, when Gustavo suddenly remembered the letter and bounded after.

"Signore! I beg of you to wait one moment. Here is a letter from ze signorina; it is come while you are away."

Tony read the address with a start of surprise.

"Then she knows!" There was regret, disillusionment, in his tone.

It was Gustavo's turn to furnish enlightenment.

"But no, signore, she do not comprehend. She sink Meestair Jayreem Ailyar is ze brover who is not arrive. She leave it for him when he come."

"Ah!" Tony ripped it open and read it through with a chuckle. He read it a second time and his face grew grave. He thrust it into his pocket and strode away without a word for Gustavo. Gustavo looked after him reproachfully. As a head waiter, he naturally did not expect to read the letters of guests; but as a fellow conspirator, he felt that he was entitled to at least a general knowledge of all matters bearing on the conspiracy. He turned back down stairs with a disappointed droop to his shoulders.

Tony closed his door and walked to the window where he stood staring at the roof of Villa Rosa. He drew the letter from his pocket and read it for the third time slowly, thoughtfully, very, very soberly. The reason was clear; she was tired of Tony and was looking ahead for fresh worlds to conquer. Jerry Junior was to come next.

He understood why she had been so complaisant today. She wished the curtain to go down on the comedy note. Tomorrow, the nameless young American, the "Abraham Lincoln" of the register, would call—by the gate—would be received graciously, introduced in his proper person to the guests; the story of the donkey-man would be recounted and laughed over, and he would be politely asked when he was planning to resume his travels. This would be the end of the episode. To Constance, it had been merely an amusing farce about which she could boast when she returned to America. In her vivacious style it would make a story, just as her first meeting with Jerry Junior had made a story. But as for the play itself, for *him*, she cared nothing. Tony the man had made no impression. He must pass on and give place to Jerry Junior.

A flush crept over Tony's face and his mouth took a straighter line as he continued to gaze down on the roof of Villa Rosa. His reflections were presently interrupted by a knock. He turned and threw the door open with a fling.

"Well?" he inquired.

Gustavo took a step backward.

"*Scusi*, signore, but zay are eating ze dessart and in five—ten minutes ze omnibus will arrive."

"The omnibus?" Tony stared. "Oh!" he laughed shortly. "I was just joking, Gustavo."

Gustavo bowed and turned down the corridor; there was a look on Tony's face that did not encourage confidences. He had not gone half a dozen steps, however, when the door opened again and Tony called him back.

"I am going away tomorrow morning—by the first boat this time—and you mustn't let my aunt and sister know. I will write two letters and you are to take them down to the steward of the boat that leaves tonight. Ask him to put on Austrian stamps and mail them at Riva, so they'll get back here tomorrow. Do you understand?"

Gustavo nodded and backed away. His disappointment this time was too keen for words. He saw stretching before him a future like the past, monotonously bereft of plots and masquerades.

Tony, having hit on a plan, sat down and put it into instant execution. Opening his Baedeker, he turned to Riva and picked out the first hotel that was mentioned. Then he wrote two letters, both short and to the point; he indulged in none of Constance's vacillations, and yet in their way his letters also were masterpieces of illusion. The first was addressed to Miss Constance Wilder at Villa Rosa. It ran:

"HOTEL SOLE D'ORO,
"RIVA, AUSTRIA.

"Dear Miss Wilder: Nothing would give me greater pleasure than spending a few days in Valedolmo, but unfortunately I am pressed for time, and am engaged to start Thursday morning with some friends on a trip through the Dolomites.

"Trusting that I may have the pleasure of making your acquaintance at some future date,

"Yours truly,

"JERYMN HILLIARD, JR."

The second letter was addressed to his sister, but he trusted to luck that Constance would see it. It ran:

"HOTEL SOLE D'ORO,
"RIVA, AUSTRIA.

"Dear Nan: Who in thunder is Constance Wilder? She wants us to stop and make a visit in Valedolmo. I wouldn't step into that infernal town, not if the king himself invited me—it's the deadest hole on the face of the earth. You can stay if you like and I'll go on through the Dolomites alone. There's an American family stopping here who are also planning the trip—a stunning girl; I know you'd like her.

"Of course the travelling will be pretty rough. Perhaps you and Aunt Kate would rather visit your friends and meet me later in Munich. If you decide to take the trip, you will have to come on down to Riva as soon as you get this letter, as we're planning to pull out Thursday morning.

"Sorry to hurry you, but you know my vacation doesn't last forever.

"Love to Aunt Kate and yourself,

"Yours ever,

"JERRY."

He turned the letters over to Gustavo with a five-franc note, leaving Gustavo to decide with his own conscience whether the money was intended for himself or the steward of the Regina Margarita. This accomplished, he slipped out unobtrusively and took the road toward Villa Rosa.

He strode along with his hands in his pockets and his eyes on the path until he nearly bumped his nose against the villa gate-post. Then he stopped and thought. He had no mind to be ushered to the terrace where he would have to dissemble some excuse for his visit before Miss Hazel and Mr. Wilder. His business tonight was with Constance, and Constance alone. He turned and skirted the villa wall, determined on reconnoitering first. There was a place in the wall—he knew well—where the stones were missing, and a view was obtainable of the terrace and parapet.

He reached the place to find Lieutenant Carlo di Ferara already there. Now the Lieutenant's purpose was exactly as innocent as Tony's own; he merely wished to assure himself that Captain Coroloni was not before him. It was considered a joke at the tenth cavalry mess to detail one or the other of the officers to call on the Americans at the same time that Lieutenant di Ferara called. He was not spying on the family, merely on his meddling brother officers.

Tony of course could know nothing of this, and as his eyes fell upon the lieutenant, there was apparent in their depths a large measure of contempt. A lieutenant in the Royal Italian Cavalry can afford to be generous in many things, but he cannot afford to swallow contempt from a donkey-driver. The signorina was not present this time; there was no reason why he should not punish the fellow. He dropped his hand on Tony's shoulder—on his collar to be exact—and whirled him about. The action was accompanied by some vigorous colloquial Italian—the gist of it being that Tony was to mind his own business and mend his manners. The lieutenant had a muscular arm, and Tony turned. But Tony had not played quarterback four years for nothing; he tackled low, and the next moment the lieutenant was rolling down the bank of a dried stream that stretched at their feet. No one likes to roll down a dusty stony bank, much less an officer in immaculate uniform on the eve of paying a formal call upon ladies. He picked himself up and looked at Tony; he was quite beyond speech.

Tony looked back and smiled. He swept off his hat with a deferential bow. "*Scusi*," he murmured, and jumped over the wall into the grounds of Villa Rosa.

The lieutenant gasped. If anything could have been more insultingly inadequate to the situation than that one word *scusi*, it did not at the moment occur to him. Jeering, blasphemy, vituperation, he might have excused, but this! The shock jostled him back to a thinking state.

Here was no ordinary donkey-driver. The hand that had rested for a moment on his arm was the hand of a gentleman. The man's face was vaguely, elusively familiar; if the lieutenant had not seen him before, he had at least seen his picture. The man had pretended he could not talk Italian, but—*scusi*—it came out very pat when it was needed.

An idea suddenly assailed Lieutenant di Ferara. He scrambled up the bank and skirted the wall, almost on a run, until he reached the place where his horse was tied. Two minutes later he was off at a gallop, headed for the house of the prefect of police of Valedolmo.

CHAPTER XVI

Tony jumped over the wall. He might have landed in the midst of a family party; but in so much luck was with him. He found the *Farfalla* bobbing at the foot of the water steps with Mr. Wilder and Miss Hazel already embarked. They were waiting for Constance, who had obligingly run back to the house to fetch the rainbow shawl (finished that afternoon) as Miss Hazel distrusted the Italian night breeze.

Constance stepped out from the door as Tony emerged from the bushes. She regarded him in startled surprise; he was still in some slight disarray from his encounter with the lieutenant.

"May I speak to you, Miss Wilder? I won't detain you but a moment."

She nodded and kept on, her heart thumping absurdly. He had received the letter of course; and there would be consequences. She paused at the top of the water steps.

"You go on," she called to the others, "and pick me up on your way back. Tony wants to see me about something, and I don't like to keep Mrs. Eustace and Nannie waiting."

Giuseppe pushed off and Constance was left standing alone on the water steps. She turned as Tony approached; there was a touch of defiance in her manner.

"Well?"

He came to her side and leaned carelessly against the parapet, his eyes on the *Farfalla* as she tossed and dipped in the wash of the *Regina Margarita* which was just puffing out from the village landing. Constance watched him, slightly taken aback; she had expected him to be angry, sulky, reproachful—certainly not nonchalant. When he finally brought his eyes from the water, his expression was mildly melancholy.

"Signorina, I have come to say good bye. It is very sad, but tomorrow, I too—" he waved his hand toward the steamer—"shall be a passenger."

"You are going away from Valedolmo?"

He nodded.

"Unfortunately, yes. I should like to stay, but—" he shrugged—"life isn't all play, Miss Wilder. Though one would like to be a donkey-man forever, one only may be for a summer's holiday. I am your debtor for a unique and pleasant experience."

She studied his face without speaking. Did it mean that he had got the letter and was hurt, or did it perhaps mean that he had got the letter and did not care to appear as Jerry Junior? That he enjoyed the play so long as he could remain incognito and stop it where he pleased, but that he had no mind to let it drift into reality? Very possibly it meant—she flushed at the thought—that he divined Nannie's plot, and refused also to consider the fourth candidate.

She laughed and dropped into their usual jargon.

"And the young American man, Signor Abraham Lincoln, will he come tomorrow for tea?"

"Ah, signorina, he is desolated, but it is not possible. He has received a letter and he must go; he has stopped too long in Valedolmo. Tomorrow morning early, he and I togever, we sail away to Austria." His eyes went back to the trail of smoke left by the little steamer.

"And Costantina, Tony. You are leaving her behind?" It took some courage to put this question, but she did not flinch; she put it with a laugh which contained nothing but raillery.

Tony sighed—a deep melodramatic sigh—and laid his hand on his heart.

"Ah, signorina, zat Costantina, she has not any heart. She love one man one day, anozzer ze next. I go away to forget."

His eyes dropped to hers; for an instant the mocking light died out; a questioning, wounded look took its place.

She felt a quick impulse to hold out her hands, to say, "Jerry, don't go!" If she only knew! Was he going because he thought that she wished to dismiss him, or because he wished to dismiss himself? Was it pique that bade him carry the play to the end, or was it merely the desire to get out of an awkward situation gracefully?

She stood hesitating, scanning the terrace pavement with troubled eyes; when she raised them to his face the chance was gone. He straightened his shoulders with an air of finality and picked up his hat from the balustrade.

"Some day, signorina, in New York, perhaps I play a little tune underneaf your window."

She nodded and smiled.

"I will give the monkey a penny when he comes—good-bye."

He bowed over her hand and touched it lightly to his lips.

"Signorina, *addio*!"

As he strode away into the dusky lane of cypresses, she heard him whistling softly "Santa Lucia." It was the last stroke, she reflected, angrily; he might at least have omitted that! She turned away and dropped down on the water steps to wait for the *Farfalla*. The terrace, the lake, the beautiful Italian night, suddenly seemed deserted and empty. Before she knew it was coming, she had leaned her head against the balustrade with a deep sob. She caught herself sharply. She to sit there crying, while Tony went whistling on his way!

* * *

As the *Farfalla* drifted idly over the water, Constance sat in the stern, her chin in her hand, moodily gazing at the shimmering path of moonlight. But no one appeared to notice her silence, since Nannie was talking enough for both. And the only thing she talked about was Jerry Junior, how funny and clever and charming he was, how phenomenally good—for a man; when she showed signs of stopping, Mr. Wilder by a question started her on. It seemed to Constance an interminable two hours before they dropped their guests in the garden of the Hotel du Lac, and headed again for Villa Rosa.

As they approached their own water steps it became apparent that someone—a man—was standing at the top in an attitude of expectancy. Constance's heart gave a sudden bound and the next instant sank deep. A babble of frenzied greetings floated out to meet them; there was no mistaking Gustavo. Moreover, there was no mistaking the fact that he was excited; his excitement was contagious even before they had learned the reason. He stuttered in his impatience to share the news.

"Signore! *Dio mio*! A calamity has happened. Zat Tony, zat donk'-man! he has got hisself arrested. Zay say it is a lie, zat he is American citizen; he is an officer who is dessert from ze Italian army. Zay say he just pretend he cannot spik Italian—but it is not true. He know ten—leven words."

They came hurrying up the steps and surrounded him, Mr. Wilder no less shocked than Gustavo himself.

"Arrested—as a deserter? It's an outrage!" he thundered.

Constance laid her hand on Gustavo's sleeve and whirled him about.

"What do you mean? I don't understand. Where is Tony?"

Gustavo groaned.

"In jail, signorina. Four carabinieri are come to take him away. And he fight—*Dio mio*! he fight like ze devil. But zay put—" he indicated handcuffs—"and he go."

Constance dropped down on the upper step and leaning her head against the balustrade, she laughed until she was weak.

Her father whirled upon her indignantly.

"Constance! Haven't you any sympathy for the man? This isn't a laughing matter."

"I know, Dad, but it's so funny—Tony an Italian officer! He can't pronounce the ten—leven words he does know right."

"Of course he can't; he doesn't know as much Italian as I do. Can't these fools tell an American citizen when they see one? I'll teach 'em to go about chucking American citizens in jail.

I'll telegraph the consul in Milan; I'll make an international matter of it!"

He fumed up and down the terrace, while Constance rose to her feet and followed after with a pretense at pacification.

"Hush, Dad! Don't be so excitable. It was a very natural mistake for them to make. But if Tony is really what he says he is it will be very easily proved. You must be sure of your ground though, before you act. I don't like to say anything against poor Tony now that he is in trouble, but I have always felt that there was a mystery connected with him. For all we know he may be a murderer or a brigand or an escaped convict in disguise. We only have his word you know that he is an American citizen."

"His word!" Mr. Wilder fairly exploded. "Are you utterly blind? He's exactly as much an American citizen as I am. He's—" He stopped and fanned himself furiously. He had sworn never to betray Tony's secret, and yet, the present situation was exceptionable.

Constance patted him on the arm.

"There, Dad. I haven't a doubt his story is true. He was born in Budapest, and he's a naturalized American citizen. It's the duty of the United States Government to protect him—but it won't be difficult; I dare say he's got his naturalization papers with him. A word in the morning will set everything straight."

"Leave him in jail all night?"

"But you can't do anything now; it's after ten o'clock; the authorities have gone to bed."

She turned to Gustavo; her tone was reassuring.

"In the morning we'll get some American war-ships to bombard the jail."

"Signorina, you joke!" His tone was reproachful.

She suddenly looked anxious.

"Gustavo, is the jail strong?"

"Ver' strong, signorina."

"He can't escape and get over into Austria? We are very near the frontier, you know."

"No, signorina, it is impossible." He shook his head hopelessly.

Constance laughed and slipped her hand through her father's arm.

"Come, Dad. The first thing in the morning we'll go down to the jail and cheer him up. There's not the slightest use in worrying any more tonight. It won't hurt Tony to be kept in—er—cold storage for a few hours—I think on the whole it will do him good!"

She nodded dismissal to Gustavo, and drew her father, still muttering, toward the house.

CHAPTER XVII

Jerry Junior's letter of regret arrived from Riva on the early mail. In the light of Constance's effusively cordial invitation, the terse formality of his reply was little short of rude; but Constance read between the lines and was appeased. The writer, plainly, was angry, and anger was a much more becoming emotion than nonchalance. As she set out with her father toward the village jail, she was again buoyantly in command of the situation. She carried a bunch of oleanders, and the pink and white egg basket swung from her arm. Their way led past the gate of the Hotel du Lac, and Mr. Wilder, being under the impression that he was enjoying a very good joke all by himself, could not forego the temptation of stopping to inquire if Mrs. Eustace and Nannie had heard any news of the prodigal. They found the two at breakfast in the courtyard, an open letter spread before them. Nannie received them with lamentations.

"We can't come to the villa! Here's a letter from Jerry wanting us to start immediately for the Dolomites—did you ever know anything so exasperating?"

She passed the letter to Constance, and then as she remembered the first sentence, made a hasty attempt to draw it back. It was too late; Constance's eyes had already pounced upon it. She read it aloud with gleeful malice.

"'Who in thunder is Constance Wilder?'—If that's an example of the famous Jerry Junior's politeness, I prefer not to meet him, thank you.—It's worse than his last insult; I shall *never* forgive this!" She glanced down the page and handed it back with a laugh; from her point of vantage it was naïvely transparent. From Mr. Wilder's point, however, the contents were inscrutable; he looked from the letter to his daughter's serene smile, and relapsed into a puzzled silence.

"I should say on the contrary, that he *doesn't* want you to start immediately for the Dolomites," Constance observed.

"It's a girl," Nannie groaned. "I suspected it from the moment we got the telegram in Lucerne. Oh, why did I ever let that wretched boy get out of my sight?"

"I dare say she's horrid," Constance put in. "One meets such frightful Americans traveling."

"We will go up to Riva on the afternoon boat and investigate." It was Mrs. Eustace who spoke. There was an undertone in her voice which suggested that she was prepared to do her duty by her brother's son, however unpleasant that duty might be.

"American girls are so grasping," said Nannie plaintively. "It's scarcely safe for an unattached man to go out alone."

Mr. Wilder leaned forward and reexamined the letter.

"By the way, Miss Nannie, how did Jerry learn that you were here? His letter, I see, was mailed in Riva at ten o'clock last night."

Nannie examined the post mark.

"I hadn't thought of that! How could he have found out—unless that beast of a head waiter telegraphed? What does it mean?"

Mr. Wilder spread out his hands and raised his shoulders. "You've got me!" A gleam of illumination suddenly flashed over his face; he turned to his daughter with what was meant to be a carelessly off-hand manner. "Er—Constance, while I think of it, you didn't discharge Tony again yesterday, did you?"

Constance opened her eyes.

"Discharge Tony? Why should I do that? He isn't working for me."

"You weren't rude to him?"

"Father, am I ever rude to anyone?"

Mr. Wilder looked at the envelope again and shook his head. "There's something mighty fishy about this whole business. When you get hold of that brother of yours again, my dear young woman, you make him tell what he's been up to this week—and make him tell the truth."

"Mr. Wilder!" Nannie was reproachful. "You don't know Jerry; he's incapable of telling anything but the truth."

Constance tittered.

"What are you laughing at, Constance?"

"Nothing—only it's so funny. Why don't you advertise for him? Lost—a young man, age twenty-eight, height, five feet eleven, weight one hundred and seventy pounds, dark hair, gray eyes, slight scar over left eye brow; dressed when last seen in double breasted blue serge suit and brown russet shoes. Finder please return to Hotel du Lac and receive liberal reward."

"He isn't lost," said Nannie. "We know where he is perfectly; he's at the Hotel Sole d' Oro in Riva, and that's at the other end of the lake. We're going up on the afternoon boat to join him."

"Oh!" said Constance, meekly.

"You take my advice," Mr. Wilder put in. "Go up to Riva if you must—it's a pleasant trip—but leave your luggage here. See this young man in person and bring him back with you; tell him we have just as good mountains as he'll find in the Dolomites. If by any chance you shouldn't find him—"

"Of course, we'll find him!" said Nannie.

Constance looked troubled.

"Don't go, it's quite a long trip. Write instead and give the letter to Gustavo; he'll give it to the boat steward who will deliver it personally. Then if Jerry shouldn't be there—"

Nannie was losing her patience.

"Shouldn't be there? But he *says* he's there."

"Oh! yes, certainly, that ends it. Only, you know, Nannie, *I* don't believe there really is any such person as Jerry Junior! I think he's a myth."

Gustavo had been hanging about the gate looking anxiously up the road as if he expected something to happen. His brow cleared suddenly as a boy on a bicycle appeared in the distance. The boy whirled into the court and dismounted; glancing dubiously from one to the other of the group, he finally presented his telegram to Gustavo, who passed it on to Nannie. She ripped it open and ran her eyes over the contents.

"Can anyone tell me the meaning of this? It's Italian!" She spread it on the table while the three bent over it in puzzled wonder.

"Ceingide mai maind dunat comtu Riva stei in Valedolmo geri."

Constance was the first to grasp the meaning; she read it twice and laughed.

"That's not Italian; it's English, only the operator has spelt it phonetically—I begin to believe there is a Jerry," she added, "no one could cause such a bother who didn't exist." She picked up the slip and translated:

"'Changed my mind. Do not come to Riva; stay in Valedolmo. Jerry.'"

"I'm a clairvoyant you see. I told you he wouldn't be there!"

"But where is he?" Nannie wailed.

Constance and her father glanced tentatively at each other and were silent. Gustavo who had been hanging officiously in the rear, approached and begged their pardon.

"*Scusi*, signora, but I sink I can explain. *Ecco*! Ze telegram is dated from Limone—zat is a village close by here on ze ozzer side of ze lake. He is gone on a walking trip, ze yong man, of two—tree days wif an Englishman who is been in zis hotel. If he expect you so soon he would not go. But patience, he will come back. Oh, yes, in a little while, after one—two day he come back."

"What is the man talking about?" Mrs. Eustace was both indignant and bewildered. "Jerry was in Riva yesterday at the Hotel Sole d' Oro. How can he be on a walking trip at the other end of the lake today?"

"You don't suppose—" Nannie's voice was tragic—"that he has eloped with that American girl?"

"Good heavens, my dear!" Mrs. Eustace appealed to Mr. Wilder. "What are the laws in this dreadful country? Don't banns or something have to be published three weeks before the ceremony can take place?"

Mr. Wilder rose hastily.

"Yes, yes, dear lady. It's impossible; don't consider any such catastrophe for a moment. Come, Constance, I really think we ought to be going.—Er, you see, Mrs. Eustace, you can't believe—that is, don't let anything Gustavo says trouble you. With all respect for his many fine qualities, he has not Jerry's regard for truth. And don't bother any more about the boy; he will turn up in a day or so. He may have written some letters of explanation that you haven't got. These foreign mails—" He edged toward the gate.

Constance followed him and then turned back.

"We're on our way to the jail," she said, "to visit our donkey-driver who has managed to get himself arrested. While we're there we can make inquiries if you like; it's barely possible that they might have got hold of Jerry on some false charge or other. These foreign jails—"

"Constance!" said Nannie reproachfully.

"Oh, my dear, I was only joking; of course it's impossible. Good bye." She nodded and laughed and ran after her father.

CHAPTER XVIII

If one must go to jail at all one could scarcely choose a more entertaining jail than that of Valedolmo. It occupies a structure which was once a palace; and its cells, planned for other purposes, are spacious. But its most gratifying feature, to one forcibly removed from social intercourse, is its outlook. The windows command the Piazza Garibaldi, which is the social center of the town; it contains the village post, the fountain, the tobacco shop, the washing-trough, and the two rival cafès, the "Independenza" and the "Libertà." The piazza is always dirty and noisy—that goes without saying—but on Wednesday morning at nine o'clock, it is peculiarly dirty and noisy. Wednesday is Valedolmo's market day, and the square is so cluttered with booths and huxters and anxious buyers, that the peaceable pedestrian can scarcely wedge his way through. The noise moreover is deafening; above the cries of vendors and buyers, rises a shriller chorus of bleating kids and squealing pigs and braying donkeys.

Mr. Wilder, red in the face and short of temper, pushed through the crowd with little ceremony, prodding on the right with his umbrella, on the left with his fan, and using his elbows vigorously. Constance, serenely cool, followed in his wake, nodding here and there to a chance acquaintance, smiling on everyone; the spectacle to her held always fresh interest. An image vendor close at her elbow insisted that she should buy a Madonna and Bambina for fifty centesimi, or at least a San Giuseppe for twenty-five. To her father's disgust she bought them both, and presented them to two wide-eyed children who in bashful fascination were dogging their footsteps.

The appearance of the foreigners in the piazza caused such a ripple of interest, that for a moment the bargaining was suspended. When the two mounted the steps of the jail and jerked the bell, as many of the bystanders as the steps would accommodate mounted with them. Nobody answered the first ring, and Constance pulled again with a force which sent a jangle of bells echoing through the interior. After a second's wait—snortingly impatient on Mr. Wilder's part; he was being pressed close by the none too clean citizens of Valedolmo—the door was opened a very small crack by a frowsy jailoress. Her eye fell first upon the crowd, and she was disposed to close it again; but in the act she caught sight of the Signorina Americana dressed in white, smiling above a bouquet of oleanders. Her eyes widened with astonishment. It was long since such an apparition had presented itself at that door. She dropped a courtesy and the crack widened.

"The two mounted the steps of the jail and jerked the bell"

"Your commands, signorina?"

"We wish to come in."

"But it is against the orders. Friday is visiting-day at thirteen o'clock. If the signorina had a *permesso* from the *sindaco*, why then—"

The signorina shook her head and shrugged her shoulders. She had no *permesso* and it was too much trouble to get one. Besides, the *sindaco's* office didn't open till ten o'clock. She glanced down; there was a shining two-franc piece in her hand. Perhaps the jailoress would allow them to step inside away from the crowd and she would explain?

This sounded reasonable; the door opened farther and they squeezed through. It banged in the faces of the disappointed spectators, who lingered hopefully a few moments longer, and then returned to their bargaining. Inside the big damp stone-walled corridor Constance drew a deep breath and smiled upon the jailoress; the jailoress smiled back. Then as a preliminary skirmish, Constance presented the two-franc piece; and the jailoress dropped a courtesy.

"We have heard that Antonio, our donkey-driver, has been arrested for deserting from the army and we have come to find out about it. My father, the signore here—" she waved her hand toward Mr. Wilder—"likes Antonio very much and is quite sure that it is a mistake."

The woman's mouth hardened; she nodded with emphasis.

"*Già*. We have him, the man Antonio, if that is his name. He may not be the deserter they search—I do not know—but if he is not the deserter he is something else. You should have heard him last night, signorina, when they brought him in. The things he said! They were in a foreign tongue; I did not understand, but I *felt*. Also he kicked my husband—kicked him quite hard so that he limps today. And the way he orders us about! You would think he were a prince in his own palace and we were his servants. Nothing is good enough for him. He objected to the room we gave him first because it smelt of the cooking. He likes butter with his bread and hot milk with his coffee. He cannot smoke the cigars which my husband bought for him, and they cost three soldi apiece. And this morning—" her voice rose shrilly as she approached the climax—"he called for a bath. It is true, signorina, a *bath. Dio mio*, he wished me to carry the entire village fountain to his room!"

"Not really?" Constance opened her eyes in shocked surprise. "But surely, signora, you did not do it?"

The woman blinked.

"It would be impossible, signorina," she contented herself with saying.

Constance, with grave concern, translated the sum of Tony's enormities to her father; and turned back to the jailoress apologetically.

"My father is very much grieved that the man should have caused you so much trouble. But he says, that if we could see him, we could persuade him to be more reasonable. We talk his language, and can make him understand."

The woman winked meaningly.

"Eh—he pretends he cannot talk Italian, but he understands enough to ask for what he wishes. I think—and the Signor-Lieutenant who ordered his arrest thinks—that he is shamming."

"It was a lieutenant who ordered his arrest? Do you remember his name—was it Carlo di Ferara?"

"It might have been." Her face was vague.

"Of the cavalry?"

"*Si*, signorina, of the cavalry—and very handsome."

Constance laughed. "Well, the plot thickens! Dad, you must come to Tony's hearing this afternoon, and put it tactfully to our friend the lieutenant that we don't like to have our donkey-man snatched away without our permission." She turned back to the jailoress. "And now, where is the man? We should like to speak with him."

"It is against the orders, but perhaps—I have already permitted the head waiter from the Hotel du Lac to carry him newspapers and cigarettes. He says that the man Antonio is in reality an American nobleman from New York who merely plays at being a donkey-driver for diversion, and that unless he is set at liberty immediately a ship will come with cannon, but—we all know Gustavo, signorina."

Constance nodded and laughed.

"You have reason! We all know Gustavo—may we go right up?"

The jailoress called the jailor. They talked aside; the two-franc piece was produced as evidence. The jailor with a great show of caution got out a bunch of keys and motioned them to follow. Up two flights and down a long corridor with peeling frescoes on the walls—nymphs and cupids and garlands of roses; most incongruous decorations for a jail—at last they paused before a heavy oak door. Their guide tried two wrong keys, swore softly as each failed to turn, and finally with an exclamation of triumph produced the right one. He swung the door wide and stepped back with a bow.

A large room was revealed, brick-floored and somewhat scanty as to furniture, but with a view—an admirable view, if one did not mind its being checked off into iron squares. The most conspicuous object in the room, however, was its occupant, as he sat, in an essentially American attitude, with his chair tipped back and his feet on the table. A cloud of tobacco smoke and a wide spread copy of a New York paper concealed him from too impertinent gaze. He did not raise his head at the sound of the opening door but contented himself with growling:

"Confound your impudence! You might at least knock before you come in."

Constance laughed and advanced a hesitating step across the threshold. Tony dropped his paper and sprang to his feet, his face assuming a shade of pink only less vivid than the oleanders. She shook her head sorrowfully.

"I don't need to tell you, Tony, how shocked we are to find you in such a place. Our trust has been rudely shaken; we had not supposed we were harboring a deserter."

Mr. Wilder stepped forward and held out his hand; there was a twinkle in his eye which he struggled manfully to suppress.

"Nonsense, Tony, we don't believe a word of it. You a deserter from the Italian army? It's preposterous! Where are your naturalization papers?"

"Thank you, Mr. Wilder, but I don't happen to have my papers with me—I trust it won't be necessary to produce them. You see—" his glance rested entirely on Mr. Wilder; he studiously overlooked Constance's presence—"this Angelo Fresi, the fellow they are after, got into a quarrel over a gambling debt and struck a superior officer. To avoid being court-martialed he lit out; it happened a month ago in Milan and they've been looking for him ever since. Now last night I had the misfortune to tip Lieutenant Carlo di Ferara over into a ditch. The matter was entirely accidental and I regretted it very much. I, of course, apologized. But what did the lieutenant do but take it into his head that I, being an assaulter of superior officers, was, by *a priori* reasoning, this Angelo Fresi in disguise. Accordingly—" he waved his hand around the room—"you see me here."

"It's an imposition! Depriving an American citizen of his liberty on any such trumped-up charge as that! I'll telegraph the consul in Milan. I'll—"

"Oh, don't trouble. I'll get off this afternoon; they've sent for someone to identify me, and if he doesn't succeed, I don't see how they can hold me. In the meantime, I'm comfortable enough."

Mr. Wilder's eye wandered about the room. "H'm, it isn't bad for a jail! Got everything you need—tobacco, papers? What's this, New York *Sun* only ten days old?" He picked it up and plunged into the headlines.

Constance turned from the window and glanced casually at Tony.

"You didn't go to Austria after all?"

"I was detained; I hope to get off tomorrow."

"Oh, before I forget it." She removed the basket from her arm and set it on the table. "Here is some lemon jelly, Tony. I couldn't remember whether one takes lemon jelly to prisoners or invalids—I've never known any prisoners before, you see. But anyway, I hope you'll like it; Elizabetta made it."

He bowed stiffly. "I beg of you to convey my thanks to Elizabetta."

"Tony!" She lowered her voice to a conspiratorial whisper and glanced apprehensively over her shoulder to see if the jailor were listening. "If by any chance they *should* identify you as that deserter, just get word to me and I will have Elizabetta bake you a veal pasty with a rope ladder and a file inside. I would have had her bake it this morning, only Wednesday is ironing-day at the villa, and she was so awfully busy—"

"This is your innings," Tony rejoined somewhat sulkily. "I hope you'll get all the entertainment you can out of the situation."

"Thank you, Tony, that's kind. Of course," she added with a plaintive note in her voice, "this must be tiresome for you; but it is a pleasant surprise for me. I was feeling very sad last night, Tony, at the thought that you were going to Austria and that I should never, never see you any more."

"I wish I knew whether there's any truth in that statement or not!"

"Any truth! I realize well, that I might search the whole world over and never find another donkey-man who sings such beautiful tenor, who wears such lovely sashes and such becoming earrings. Why, Tony—" she took a step nearer and her face assumed a look of consternation. "You've lost your earrings!"

He turned his back and walked to the window where he stood moodily staring at the market. Constance watched his squared shoulders dubiously out of the corner of her eye; then she glanced momentarily into the hall where the jailor was visible, his face flattened against the bars of an open window; and from him to her father, still deep in the columns of his paper, oblivious to both time and place. She crossed to Tony and stood at his side peering down at the scene below.

"I don't suppose it will interest you," she said in an off-hand tone, her eyes still intent on the crowd, "but I got a letter this morning from a young man who is stopping at the Sole d' Oro in Riva—a very rude letter I thought."

He whirled about.

"You know!"

"It struck me that the person who wrote it was in a temper and might afterwards be sorry for having hurt my feelings, and so"—she raised her eyes momentarily to his—"the invitation is still open."

"Tell me," there was both entreaty and command in his tone, "did you know the truth before you wrote that letter?"

"You mean, did I know whom I was inviting? Assuredly! Do you think it would have been dignified to write such an informal invitation to a person I did not know?"

She turned away quickly and laid her hand on her father's shoulder.

"Come, Dad, don't you think we ought to be going? Poor Tony wants to read the paper himself."

Mr. Wilder came back to the jail and his companions with a start.

"Oh, eh, yes, I think perhaps we ought. If they don't let you out this afternoon, Tony, I'll make matters lively for 'em, and if there's anything you need send word by Gustavo—I'll be back later." He fished in his pockets and brought up a handful of cigars. "Here's something better than lemon jelly, and they're not from the tobacco shop in Valedolmo either."

He dropped them on the table and turned toward the door; Constance followed with a backward glance.

"Good-bye, Tony; don't despair. Remember that it's always darkest before the dawn, and that whatever others think, Costantina and I believe in you. *We* know that you are incapable of telling anything but the truth!" She had almost reached the door when she became aware of the flowers in her hand; she hurried back. "Oh, I forgot! Costantina sent these with her—with—" She faltered; her audacity did not go quite that far.

Tony reached for them. "With what?" he insisted.

She laughed; and a second later the door closed behind her. He stood staring at the door till he heard the key turn in the lock, then he looked down at the flowers in his hand. A note was tied to the stems; his fingers trembled as he worked with the knot.

"*Caro Antonio mio*," it commenced; he could read that. "*La sua Costantina*," it ended; he could read that. But between the two was an elusive, tantalizing hiatus. He studied it and put it in his pocket and took it out and studied it again. He was still puzzling over it half an hour later when Gustavo came to inquire if the signore had need of anything.

Had he need of anything! He sent Gustavo flying to the stationer's in search of an Italian-English dictionary.

* * *

It was four o'clock in the afternoon and all the world—except Constance—was taking a siesta. The *Farfalla*, anchored at the foot of the water steps in a blaze of sunshine, was dipping up and down in drowsy harmony with the lapping waves; she was for the moment abandoned, Giuseppe being engaged with a nap in the shade of the cypress trees at the end of the drive. He was so very engaged that he did not hear the sound of an approaching carriage, until the horse was pulled to a sudden halt to avoid stepping on him. Giuseppe staggered sleepily to his feet and rubbed his eyes. He saw a gentleman descend, a gentleman clothed as for a wedding, in a frock coat and a white waistcoat, in shining hat and pearl gray gloves and a boutonnière of oleander. Having paid the driver and dismissed the carriage, the gentleman fumbled in his pocket for his card-case. Giuseppe hurrying forward with a polite bow, stopped suddenly and blinked. He fancied that he must still be dreaming; he rubbed his eyes and stared again, but he found the second inspection more confounding than the first. The gentleman looked back imperturbably, no slightest shade of recognition in his glance, unless a gleam of amusement far, far down in the depths of his eye might be termed recognition. He extracted a card with grave deliberation and handed it to his companion.

"*Voglio vedere la Signorina Costantina,*" he remarked.

The tone, the foreign accent, were both reminiscent of many a friendly though halting conversation. Giuseppe stared again, appealingly, but the gentleman did not help him out; on the contrary he repeated his request in a slightly sharpened tone.

"*Si, signore,*" Giuseppe stammered. "*Prego di verire. La signorina è nel giardino.*"

He started ahead toward the garden, looking behind at every third step to make sure that the gentleman was still following, that he was not merely a figment of his own sleepy senses. Their direction was straight toward the parapet where, on a historic wash-day, the signorina had sat beside a row of dangling stockings. She was sitting there now, dressed in white, the oleander tree above her head enveloping her in a glowing and fragrant shade. So occupied was she with a dreamy contemplation of the mountains across the lake that she did not hear footsteps until Giuseppe paused before her and presented the card. She glanced from this to the visitor and extended a friendly hand.

"Mr. Hilliard! Good afternoon."

There was nothing of surprise in her greeting; evidently she did not find the visit extraordinary. Giuseppe stared, his mouth and eyes at their widest, until the signorina dismissed him; then he turned and walked back—staggered back almost—never before, not even late at night on Corpus Domini day, had he had such overwhelming reason to doubt his senses.

"Never before had he had such overwhelming reason to doubt his senses"

Constance turned to the visitor and swept him with an appreciative glance, her eye lingering a second on the oleander in his buttonhole.

"Perhaps you can tell me, is Tony out of jail? I am so anxious to know."

He shook his head.

"Found guilty and sentenced for life; you'll never see him again."

"Ah; poor Tony! I shall miss him."

"I shall miss him too; we've had very good times together."

Constance suddenly became aware that her guest was still standing; she moved along and made place on the wall. "Won't you sit down? Oh, excuse me," she added with an anxious glance at his clothes, "I'm afraid you'll get dusty; it would be better to bring a chair." She nodded toward the terrace.

He sat down beside her.

"I am only too honored; the last time I came you did not invite me to sit on the wall."

"I am sorry if I appeared inhospitable, but you came so unexpectedly, Mr. Hilliard."

"Why 'Mr. Hilliard'? When you wrote you called me 'dear Jerry'."

"That was a slip of the pen; I hope you will excuse it."

"When I wrote I called you 'Miss Wilder'; that was a slip of the pen too. What I meant to say was 'dear Constance'."

She let this pass without comment.

"I have an apology to make."

"Yes?"

"Once, a long time ago, I insulted you; I called you a kid. I take it back; I swallow the word. You were never a kid."

"Oh," she dimpled, and then, "I don't believe you remember a thing about it!"

"Connie Wilder, a little girl in a blue sailor suit, and two nice fat braids of yellow hair dangling down her back with red bows on the ends—very convenient for pulling."

"You are making that up. You don't remember."

"Ah, but I do! And as for the racket you were making that afternoon, it was, if you will permit the expression, *infernal.* I remember it distinctly; I was trying to cram for a math. exam."

"It wasn't I. It was your bad little sisters and brothers and cousins."

"It was you, dear Constance. I saw you with my own eyes; I heard you with my own ears."

"Bobbie Hilliard was pulling my hair."

"I apologize on his behalf, and with that we will close the incident. There is something much more important which I wish to talk about."

"Have you seen Nannie?" She offered this hastily not to allow a pause.

"Yes, dear Constance, I have seen Nannie."

"Call me 'Miss Wilder' please."

"I'll be hanged if I will! You've been calling me Tony and Jerry and anything else you chose ever since you knew me—and long before for the matter of that."

Constance waived the point.

"Was she glad to see you?"

"She's always glad to see me."

"Oh, don't be so provoking! Give me the particulars. Was she surprised? How did you explain the telegrams and letters and Gustavo's stories? I should think the Hotel Sole d'Oro at Riva and the walking trip with the Englishman must have been difficult."

"Not in the least; I told the truth."

"The truth! Not all of it?"

"Every word."

"How could you?" There was reproach in her accent.

"It did come hard; I'm a little out of practice."

"Did you tell her about—about me?"

"I had to, Constance. When it came to the necessity of squaring all of Gustavo's yarns, my imagination gave out. Anyway, I had to tell her out of self-defence; she was so superior. She said it was just like a man to muddle everything up. Here I'd been ten days in the same town with the most charming girl in the world, and hadn't so much as discovered her name; whereas if *she* had been managing it—You see how it was; I had to let her know that I was quite capable of taking care of myself without any interference from her. I even—anticipated a trifle."

"How?"

"She said she was engaged. I told her I was too."

"Indeed!" Constance's tone was remote. "To whom?"

"The most charming girl in the world."

"May I ask her name?"

He laid his hand on his heart in a gesture reminiscent of Tony. "Costantina."

"Oh! I congratulate you."

"Thank you—I hoped you would."

She looked away, gravely, toward the Maggiore rising from the midst of its clouds. His gaze followed hers, and for three minutes there was silence. Then he leaned toward her.

"Constance, will you marry me?"

"No!"

A pause of four minutes during which Constance stared steadily at the mountain. At the end of that time her curiosity overcame her dignity; she glanced at him sidewise. He was watching her with a smile, partly of amusement, partly of something else.

"Dear Constance, haven't you had enough of play, are you never going to grow up? You are such a kid!"

She turned back to the mountain.

"I haven't known you long enough," she threw over her shoulder.

"Six years!"

"One week and two days."

"Through three incarnations."

She laughed a delicious rippling laugh of surrender, and slipped her hand into his.

"You don't deserve it, Jerry, after the fib you told your sister, but I think—on the whole—I will."

Neither noticed that Mr. Wilder had stepped out from the house and was strolling down the cypress alley in their direction. He rounded the corner in front of the parapet, and as his eye fell upon them, came to a startled halt. The young man failed to let go of her hand, and Constance glanced at her father with an apprehensive blush.

"Here's—Tony, Dad. He's out of jail."

"I see he is."

She slipped down from the wall and brought Jerry with her.

"We'd like your parental blessing, please. I'm going to marry him, but don't look so worried. He isn't really a donkey-man nor a Magyar nor an orphan nor an organ-grinder nor—any of the things he has said he was. He is just a plain American man and an *awful liar*!"

The young man held out his hand and Mr. Wilder shook it.

"Jerry," he said, "I don't need to tell you how pleased—"

"'Jerry!'" echoed Constance. "Father, you knew?"

"Long before you did, my dear." There was a suggestion of triumph in Mr. Wilder's tone.

"Jerry, you told." There was reproach, scorn, indignation in hers.

Jerry spread out his hands in a gesture of repudiation.

"What could I do? He asked my name the day we climbed Monte Maggiore; naturally, I couldn't tell him a lie."

"Then we haven't fooled anybody. How unromantic!"

"Oh, yes," said Jerry, "we've fooled lots of people. Gustavo doesn't understand, and Giuseppe, you noticed, looked rather dazed. Then there's Lieutenant Carlo di Ferara—"

"Oh!" said Constance, her face suddenly blank.

"You can explain to him now," said her father, peering through the trees.

A commotion had suddenly arisen on the terrace—the rumble of wheels, the confused mingling of voices. Constance and Jerry looked too. They found the yellow omnibus of the Hotel du Lac, its roof laden with luggage, drawn up at the end of the driveway, and Mrs. Eustace and Nannie on the point of descending. The center of the terrace was already occupied by Lieutenant di Ferara, who, with heels clicked together and white gloved hands at salute, was in the act of achieving a military bow. Miss Hazel fluttering from the door, in one breath welcomed the guests, presented the lieutenant, and ordered Giuseppe to convey the luggage upstairs. Then she glanced questioningly about the terrace.

"I thought Constance and her father were here—Giuseppe!"

Giuseppe dropped his end of a trunk and approached. Miss Hazel handed him the lieutenant's card. "The signorina and the signore—in the garden, I think."

Giuseppe advanced upon the garden. Jerry's face, at the sight, became as blank as Constance's. The two cast upon each other a glance of guilty terror, and from this looked wildly behind for a means of escape. Their eyes simultaneously lighted on the break in the garden wall. Jerry sprang up and pulled Constance after him. On the top, she gathered her skirts together preparatory to jumping, then turned back for a moment toward her father.

"Dad," she called in a stage whisper, "you go and meet him like a gentleman. Tell him you are very sorry, but your daughter is not at home today."

The two conspirators scrambled down on the other side; and Mr. Wilder with a sigh, dutifully stepped forward to greet the guests.

www.ingramcontent.com/pod-product-compliance
Lightning Source LLC
LaVergne TN
LVHW051004080826
845145LV00009B/2448